A Bloody Stiletto, Cold Lasagna, and a Bestseller

An Anna Romano Mystery Series

Book Two

Cheryl Denise Bannerman

PRINT ISBN: 978-1-7353352-9-2

AUDIOBOOK FORMAT:

Retail ISBN: 9781664903814

Library ISBN: 9781664903814

This is a work of fiction. All of the characters, names, incidents, organizations, and dialogue in this novel are either the products of the author's imagination or are used fictitiously.

Table of Contents

Prologue

Anna

I had just pulled the lasagna out of the oven when my phone rang. It was Shirlene. She was checking on me again for the tenth time this week. I guess she was as surprised as me that I was tangled up in yet another criminal investigation. She knew how stubborn I could be and wanted me to lay low and follow John's instructions to stay out of the investigation. I couldn't believe how stingy he had been with information on the case the past few days. It just didn't seem fair. I mean, I did find the first body. Geez.

"Don't mess this up! John is one of the good ones," Shirlene said as if scolding a small child.

"I won't, don't worry," I responded as I hung up the call.

Famous last words of a nosy Italian woman. Ha!

I wrapped the lasagna in my insulated food carry bag to keep it warm and headed for the car humming to myself.

I plugged in the address I retrieved from my internet search to Sherman Atkinson's home and started on my way.

I was rehearsing what I was going to say to him when the GPS told me I had arrived at my destination. I pulled into the long driveway and stared up at the large two-story home in awe. I was gathering my bags in the front seat when Mark stepped out of the front door and headed towards my car.

I stepped out to greet him and he offered to help me with the bags.

"Oh no, I'm fine. Thank you. Just brought a little something to say how sorry I am about your mom. How are you holding up?"

"Okay, I guess. Just heading to a friend's house. My dad's inside. Thank you for the food, it smells great," he replied as he walked to his car and got inside. Such a polite young man, I thought to myself.

I waved as he pulled off and was startled to find Sherman Atkinson at the door watching.

"Mr. Atkinson. How are you? I was just dropping off a pan of lasagna for you and your son for after the funeral tomorrow. I know cooking is the last thing on your mind when these things happen. I'm so sorry about your wife," I said, a bit awkwardly.

"That's very nice of you, Ms. Romano, right? You were the one that discovered her body in the bathroom at the charity ball," he seemed to confirm and question at the same time.

I nodded with empathy. "Yes, it was such a terrible thing that happened to her."

"Aren't you also that detective's girlfriend?" he asked, as we walked to the door and he graciously took the pan out of my hands.

"Well, yes, but…yes, I am."

As we entered the foyer and walked towards the kitchen, I looked around at the beautiful designs. Marble floors, exquisite art, abstract sculptures… "Was your wife the decorator of the house?" I asked in awe. "It's so beautiful!"

"Yes, it was one of her many hobbies. She enjoyed collecting antiques and visited auctions quite a bit," he smiled to himself.

As he was taking the pan out of the carry bag, and placing it in the fridge, his cell phone chirped. Suddenly, his facial features changed, and he turned to me with a furrowed brow. "Why don't you tell me the real reason you are here, Ms. Romano."

Just then, my phone chirped.

John texted: *Hey. Where are you?*

I responded: *Don't be mad at me…dropping off pan of lasagna at Mr. Atkinson's house.*

John replied: *He's a suspect in the murders. GET OUT NOW!*

John's text is the last thing I remember before feeling a cold knife pressed to my neck.

CHAPTER 1

On The Lady in Red...With a Touch of Flowers

Anna

I must say, everything has been going quite well with my handsome detective. The biological clock has officially stopped ticking. I actually have a real life, with a real romance, and a real future. John and I have been dating for a little over a month and tonight is our first date out in public.

I've decided to wear this new dress I picked up last week. It's a cute little red dress with white flower details that have a touch of yellow inside each flower.

I added a bit of red lipstick and a spritz of my favorite perfume before heading into the living room to see if John was dressed and ready to go. I smiled as I noted his personal items scattered about the room. A shirt here, a jacket there, his duffel bag in the corner. For some reason, it gave me a personal sense of security without feeling smothered. I liked having him here for most of the week and then back to his apartment for a few days.

He was on a call (on speaker) when I entered the room, so I smiled and quietly did a twirl in front of him, showing off my new duds. He mouthed the word 'wow' and put his index finger up to indicate 'one minute'.

Apparently, the DA wanted to confirm John's testimony for an upcoming trial this week. The attorney for the defendant was going to do his best to twist John's words making it seem like he and Billings did *not* have probable cause to enter the premises, and that the gun they found was *not* in plain sight. I admired his dedication to the job. Dealing with criminals, attorneys, and trials could be extremely stressful.

He ended the call and looked up at me from the couch.

"Wowsers! You look absolutely beautiful, Anna!" John exclaimed.

He was always so flattering. I blushed and asked if he was ready to go. Our reservation was at seven, and it was already half past six. Although the restaurant was not far away, we just never knew how traffic was going to be on Route 1.

John was dressed in a pair of navy slacks and a white dress shirt. He was just reaching for his suit jacket when the phone rang again.

"Solace."

Silence.

"Listen Billings, can we talk about this in the morning, I'm kind of in the middle of something…Okay, thanks. Bye."

My important and handsome man of law enforcement was shaking his head and apologizing as we headed out the door. I was secretly hoping he put his phone on 'do not disturb' for the rest of the evening.

It was my first time experimenting with a new cuisine with John. Since I could easily make Italian at home, it seemed silly to go out to an Italian restaurant.

John was eager to introduce me to Thai food, and despite my aversion to spicy flavors, I agreed. He said he knew the perfect place right up the road.

We were seated by the fireplace in the rear of the main dining area. Grinning from ear-to-ear, we stared into each other's eyes, tasting authentic Thai cuisines from each other's plates and sipping wine. I decided on *Tom Kha Kai* (chicken in coconut soup) and *Pad Krapow Moo Saap* (fried basil and pork), while John went for dishes with a higher spice level, *Tom Yum Goong* (spicy shrimp soup) and *Gaeng Keow Wan Kai* (green chicken curry).

We were in the middle of an intense conversation about dessert in bed when we were interrupted by a female voice who was not our waitress.

"John? John Solace?" the woman said, as she approached our table.

John looked up confused, and then he suddenly recognized the face. "Francine? Oh my goodness. How are you?"

The woman responded with open arms as John stood up to complete the embrace.

Apparently, they knew each other from Newark…when he was married to Martha. Awkwarrrrrrd.

They spent a brief moment reminiscing about old times, and she expressed her condolences about Martha. She and her husband, Martin, were just visiting family in Hamilton and this place had come highly recommended, so they stopped for dinner. Martin was out getting the car to pull around to the front, while she used the restroom. Martha headed for the front doors after letting us know she couldn't wait to tell Martin who she'd run into.

Confession: I felt immensely proud when John introduced me as his girlfriend. I was definitely blushing.

He wrapped up the spontaneous meet-and-greet and turned his attention back to date night.

"I'm so sorry about that, Anna. What are the chances of running into someone who knew me back then when…you know…I was…um," he stumbled awkwardly.

"It's okay, John. We both had lives before we met. We both have pasts. She seemed like a nice lady," I replied. Although, I was thinking to myself how the reminder of his wife and being new to dating may be triggering second thoughts about our relationship.

"Not as nice, and sweet, and beautiful, and talented, and tremendously sexy as the woman in front of me," John said seductively while he gently kissed the top of my hand.

"Check!" I said aloud as I flagged the waitress.

It was time for dessert…at home…hopefully by the fireplace. And I don't mean cannoli. It was time to make this relationship official. We had been putting it off for weeks.

Cheers to new experiences! I thought to myself, as I gulped down my last bit of wine.

Chapter 2

Get Your Ticket at the Deli

Anna

Why do I feel like I never visit the grocery store for myself? Once again, the list is 75% cat supplies and 25% cold cuts and toiletries for John and me. My babies are just plain spoiled.

I'd grown accustomed to a few stares now and then, because of my author status, but lately, everyone wants to ask me about the kidnapping case with Frederick Talon. Unfortunately, it had been all over the news.

"Excuse me," a voice behind me beckoned.

I turned to see who it was, but I didn't recognize the woman.

"I'm sorry to bother you, but aren't you that author who was kidnapped last month?" she asked.

"Yes, I am," I answered.

"My goodness, that man was horrible. And the way you escaped in that boat explosion, oh my! I'm so glad you're okay now," she sympathized, placing her hand on her chest in relief. She leaned in closer and disclosed in a soft whisper, "You know, I'm actually quite a big fan of your novels."

"Well thank you, and yes, it was quite an adventure. Thank you for your kind words."

I managed to escape the woman's additional inquiries and rushed up to the deli counter to grab a ticket and wait my turn. The line was already seven people deep when I arrived. Busy morning for cold cuts. Maybe it was national picnic week or something.

I was just about to delve into an article from a magazine I grabbed on the way in about the latest star headed to rehab when I heard a loud ruckus from the front of the store.

Being the nosy author-cat lady that I am, I headed to aisle three to get a front-row view…

> *"You crossed the line planning your annual BBQ on my birthday, bitch! You knew we were going away to the cabin that weekend!"*

> *"How dare you! Hey, wait a minute, are you wearing my tennis bracelet? You give that back! It doesn't belong to you! It was a Christmas present from MY HUSBAND last year!"*

> *"Not a chance! He gave it to me because he loves me! Face it, your marriage is washed up, sweetie!"*

> *"You wish! My husband loves me! You're just another notch in his belt. He uses dumb sluts like you for entertainment! Now give me that bracelet!"*

> *"Hey, get off of me, psycho! No wonder he sleeps around!"*

The woman in the loud makeup, tight leather pants and heels pushed the woman in the blazer, jeans, and loafers hard when she tried to grab her bracelet.

The catfight was on.

I watched the fight as if in slow motion as the two women fought and the store manager unsuccessfully tried to break them up while calling 911.

A cereal display for Buncha Oats went flying everywhere as they crashed their way to the floor. It looked like the blazer lady was no match for the loud makeup/leather pants lady. She was trying to defend herself with a baguette, but was losing the battle.

The older men in the store were staring with intensity, hoping they would catch something that resembled skin in the catfight, but were quickly disappointed.

Makeup/leather pants lady was taking off her stiletto and raising her arm above her head.

Once again, the store manager stepped in and was finally able to pull makeup/leather pants off of blazer lady. They were both notified the police were on their way and would be detained until then.

What are the odds of me getting a front-row seat to *A Woman Scorned* while picking up litter and cold cuts? Coming to a theatre near you! Ha!

The irony is, it sounded just like the funny scenarios I encounter in my Dear Jesse column. Why do women continue to fight over these cheating men? I just do not understand.

I returned to the deli counter to find I had missed my number being called and had to take another ticket. Ugh!

The crowd had dissipated at the front, and I was finally in the checkout line talking to Irma, my favorite 'senior' cashier. She was telling me about one of her grandchildren scoring a touchdown in a recent football game when I saw John pull up in the squad car out front. I watched him stroll in; the sight of him triggered memories of our intimate night before, in slow motion.

He is not going to like being thrown this case, but I guess duty calls. I waved him over to my register.

Irma seemed annoyed that I interrupted her story, but grinned when she realized who I was waving to. She somehow seemed to figure out the detective and I were an item and gave me a sly thumbs up gesture.

She was one of many people in my life who knew my age and was hoping I would marry and produce offspring *sooner* rather than *later*.

Catfight in Aisle 3

John

I hate when the department is short-staffed. Some type of 'flu bug' was going around. Billings was the first one to call in sick.

Although, lately, I actually didn't mind riding alone on the day shift. I get to daydream about Anna and how well things are going with us. Our date went so great that we consummated our relationship that night by the fireplace…with cannoli, of course. It was the perfect ending to a perfect evening.

However, running into Martha's old friend, Francine, was really awkward. I was glad Martin was outside, that guy was always so arrogant. Every time Martha and I double-dated with those two, he made it a point to humiliate the wait staff. I guess that's what happens when you come from money.

Anna handled herself perfectly. A true lady. Although, I could tell she was wondering if running into Francine had triggered feelings about Martha. I would be lying to myself if I said it didn't. Martha was a large part of my life, and I loved her very much. I'll never forget her, but I had to move on.

Anna is a wonderful woman, and any guy would be lucky to have her. I trust her with my heart and pray she doesn't hurt me. Even the guys at the station like her and that's saying a lot, as they are quite protective.

Since it's kind of slow this morning, I have time to head to my favorite café for a double espresso mocha latte with whipped cream. What the heck, you only live once, right? Just then, the radio squawked. An altercation at the local market. Figures. Right when my mouth was watering for caffeine.

It was the supermarket by Anna's house where she frequently got her litter and those special cans of cat feasts. What could possibly be going on in the daytime at the grocery store? Was somebody upset that they ran out of pastrami? I made a u-turn in the middle of the intersection and headed that way.

I was strolling in the front door when the store manager flagged me down and ushered me towards the front office. At the same time, I noticed Anna at a register waving. I waved back and gave her the 'one-minute' gesture. She knew I had to address the situation, whatever that was, first.

I'm just relieved *Anna* wasn't the situation, or in the middle of it somehow. I am learning that trouble seems to follow my rosebud everywhere. Which is why I stick close by, of course.

The manager introduced himself as Stanley Porchini and was talking extremely fast for a small, frail man. He looked to be about fifty, maybe five foot four in height and was attempting to hide his balding problem with the infamous comb-over technique. He wore burgundy wireframed glasses, a white store-monogrammed polo shirt, and beige khakis with sensible, rubber-soled shoes.

His explanation for the call went like this…

> "I was stocking melons in produce when I heard yelling from the front of the store near the registers. I heard screaming and gasps from customers as I ran towards two women wrestling on the floor. My cereal display was ruined! And the one in the leather pants was about to connect her shoe with Mrs. Atkinson's head if I hadn't stopped her! I separated the two and called 911. Apparently, the woman that attacked Mrs. Atkinson is having an affair with her husband. That's all I know, really."

When the story was finished, I stepped through the door to his office to get statements from both women. I had the name of the victim from the store manager. She was a frequent shopper at the market. To avoid drama, Stanley put the other woman in the break room next to his office. Lacking security at this location, he had no way to restrain the aggressor until the police showed up, and due to his size and stature, I doubted he was up for the confrontation anyway.

Mrs. Atkinson was sitting in the office with her head down on the desk. She raised her head when we walked in and instantly began demanding to press charges against her attacker. She had a Band-Aid on her arm and was now holding a bag of ice to her head. I offered to call her an ambulance, but she declined.

After calming her down, getting her statement, and collecting her contact information, I moved to the room next door to get the other woman's account.

There was only one problem. She was gone.

I can't say I would stick around either if I were in her shoes.

Stanley cursed himself for not restraining her, blaming recent budget cuts, and not having better security. Even the cameras in the front of the store were non-functional.

"Oh, this is all my fault. Mrs. Atkinson is never going to forgive me. Never!" Stanley exclaimed aloud while pacing the linoleum.

"It's not your fault, sir. We'll find her, don't worry," I reassured him.

It took another round of calming the manager and Mrs. Atkinson down before I could exit the office. It was going to be a long day for sure.

After speaking to some of the store patrons, *including my girlfriend*, I was able to get a vivid description of the woman for my BOLO alert. Billings felt it necessary and amusing to text me all the inside jokes from the precinct about my call. *Catfight Cleanup in Aisle 3*, *The Buncha Oats Brawl*, and *The Baguette Beatdown*. I would have found all of them amusing if I had some caffeine in my system. Unfortunately, I did not.

I walked Anna out to her car and kissed her gently on the cheek – only because it seemed we had an audience pointing and giggling in our direction through the large glass windows. Now that our relationship is public, many people who had no idea we were dating are quite shocked. That's the only downfall of living in such a small town – gossip spreads quickly. They were probably wondering how an average guy like me could snag this famous, smokin' hot, Italian woman.

As I watched Anna drive away, I was thinking about what unique cuisine my rosebud would be creating tonight; which also reminded me I was starving.

I needed to head back to the coffee shop for that latte…and a bagel. And I better make it quick, before the radio squawked again!

Chapter 4

Everyone Hates Jesse

Anna

'Whew! What a morning,' I thought to myself as I unpacked the groceries. I noticed Sonny was not with everyone else in the living room and figured he must be up to no good. I'll check the bathroom and back bedrooms in a minute. Tiny hadn't been feeling well this week, with some type of stomach bug, and was not his usual hyper self. The others just left him alone to lick his wounds.

Tonight, I was excited to try a new recipe for *pasta e fagioli with escarole*. I was also baking some pistachio and dried cherry biscotti to go with John's morning coffee. Of course, making an extra ziplock bag for his partner, Billings, was a must.

Time to start the pot and bring the initial ingredients to a boil. I was trying to concentrate on the pasta, but couldn't get that incident in the grocery store out of my head. It sounded so familiar. I put the pot on low and headed to my laptop. Just then, I remembered that Sonny was MIA and made a detour towards the back rooms. The doors were shut, so I headed down the hall to the bathroom.

That's when I saw it. I had only myself to blame. I was the one who left the door open. The entire floor was covered in shredded toilet paper.

I yelled and scolded, but I don't think he really cared.

After cleaning up the mess, I headed back to the laptop. Jasmine was right there ready to type with me. I shooed her off the keyboard, opened up my Dear Jesse folder, and then opened the subfolder for last week.

I did a keyword search for *cheating* and *mistress*, but too many documents popped up in the results. After the morning

I'd had, I didn't know if I'd have the patience to scroll through each one individually, but hey, what the heck, I'll give it a try.

It wasn't until I got to the seventh letter in the search results that I perked up. This may be the one!

A wife had suspected her husband of having an affair. Some of her jewelry was missing, and she wanted to know if she should confront him. The only thing she knew about this woman was that her initials were M.L. I'm not sure how she found this out. Maybe the husband had the mistress's initials monogrammed on something and charged it to his credit card. It happens to be how most men get caught…the infamous paper trail. The letter was signed *Tired of the Lies*.

I re-read what I wrote back to her:

> *Hey, Tired of the Lies!*
>
> *Thanks for reaching out to Dear Jesse. It sounds like you have your hands full with your husband. I'm assuming this isn't the first time he's caused you heartache.*
>
> *You know what they say, if you accept the same behaviors over and over, nothing will change. I think you should confront the SOB and then take him for every cent he's worth in a long, drawn-out divorce!*
>
> *He doesn't deserve you! And what's up with the missing jewelry? Is he selling it off or stowing it away for his other girlfriend(s)?*
>
> *When you find out who she is, you should thank her for letting you know what a sleaze*

> *your husband is by taking her out to dinner! Now that would drive him crazy for sure!*
>
> *From Jesse's typewriter to your mailbox…that's my advice and I'm sticking to it!*

> *Yours truly,*
>
> *Jesse*

This could definitely be a match to the altercation between the wife and the mistress in the store today.

Well, since my pot was on low for the moment, what harm would it do to do some casual research on Google. How many women with the initials M.L. live in our small town anyway? Surely, everyone has a social media page in this day and age, right? I already knew what she looked like. Who could forget those leather pants! Ha!

My cell phone chirped, and I looked down at the text message.

> **John**: *Hey rosebud, you staying out of trouble?*

> **Me**: *Absolutely honeybun. Just making you a fabulous dinner for tonight! Muah!*

> **John**: *Sounds great! See you tonight.*

I put my phone away and thought to myself 'A little white lie never hurt anybody… right?'

Chapter 5

Go Bake Somethin'!

John

I was looking forward to dinner with Anna, but it would have to be a short meal. One of the night-shift detectives called in sick, and I offered to cover for him. I hoped this bug going around wouldn't get me next. I hate being sick.

I pulled up to the curb only to find Mr. Craigly on the sidewalk in front of the house talking to Anna.

"Evening, Mr. Craigly. How are you feeling? Anna told me you had a tumble last week."

"Yeah, yeah, I'm fine," he grumbled. "I heard you broke up a catfight today."

He seemed anxious to hear the details, like he was going to start rubbing his hands together and licking his lips in anticipation of a juicy story.

"Well, I'm glad you're okay. And, yes, there was an altercation at the market today. I'm still on the case, so I can't discuss any details though," I responded gently.

"Yeah, I know the drill. My buddy Ray told me all about it. Said there were articles of clothing flying everywhere. Sorry I missed it!" he chuckled slyly.

Anna was gesturing me inside quickly.

"Okay, you have a nice night, Mr. Craigly."

He shrugged as usual and rolled away on his motor scooter. Anna waved goodbye and yelled after him to come by in the morning for some biscotti.

I smirked and mentioned something about none being left for him under my breath.

Anna had outdone herself with dinner. With the exception of the Italian bread, the dish was very healthy, with tons of veggies. I had been trying to drop a few pounds lately around the old waistline. Anna's cooking was great, but those pounds add up on the scale quickly. I don't know how she stays so petite. Good metabolism, I guess.

During dinner, Anna told me how she had the best description of the leather-pants woman and that she could recite the whole argument, word-for-word, in case I needed her to testify in court. I immediately put my hand up and told her that wouldn't be necessary and to please stay out of it.

Anna had enough excitement in the last couple of months to last her a lifetime, and as her boyfriend now, I took it as my personal duty to keep her safe.

There was no way I was going to tell her that the identity of the mistress in leather pants had been confirmed. The less she knew, the better.

As she was preparing my thermos with coffee, she proceeded to tell me about the similarities between the letter sent to her *Dear Jesse* column and my case. She also told me about the initials of the mistress, M.L. With her resources, and mine too, she offered to track the sender of the letter and find out who the mistress was…for me, of course. Obviously, my message was not getting through to her.

I reminded her that she is an author, a writer, a caregiver of seven wonderful cats…but not a detective. I will handle the investigative work from now on, and she is NOT to get involved under ANY circumstances.

She protested, "Not even Googling or visiting the reference section at the library?"

"Nope! Not even that. Promise me, Anna." I gave her my harshest stare, trying not to smile because she was just too adorable.

"I promise," she said while sighing heavily.

Little did I know, her fingers were crossed behind her back when she answered me.

Gossip Is My Middle Name

Anna

As soon as John left, I rushed to my laptop. He didn't say anything about email or chat, so I still had those options left open for snooping.

And I knew just who to ping: Chatty Cathy Morton, the town gossip. If she didn't have information about the latest happenings, nobody did!

I met Cathy last year at a Christmas party. She was more than willing to swap contact info with a 'famous person' as she called me. Actually, I found her animated demeanor quite entertaining. It matched her strawberry blonde hair, large hoop earrings, red spandex dress, and fancy cowboy boots. I'm almost positive there was a matching cowboy hat at home. She was originally from Texas, having moved to New Jersey a few years ago for a job.

I clicked on her ID, cathym69. Don't ask. I'm sure it's just her birth year.

I typed in the box: *Hey Cathy! What's up?*

She responded right away. I could hear her Southern accent coming through in her response.

> **Cathy**: *Hey Famous Lady! Nothing much. Just giving myself a pedicure. Word around town is you and that detective were making out in the market parking lot this morning! Such a bad girlllll!*

> **Me**: *We were NOT making out, that's ridiculous. Anyway...you heard about the fight at the market, right?*

Cathy: *Heard about it! That's all anyone's been talking about! That poor woman having to face yet another one of her husband's mistresses. That no-good, cheatin' bastard!*

Me: *Totally! So you know her?*

Cathy: *Who doesn't! She and her husband are like royalty in Princeton and up in Montclair. All the areas where the well-to-do congregate. She shops at the same market as you all the time. You never bumped into her?*

Me: *Oh wow, okay. No, I must go at a different time than she does. I was running late this morning. So, what's her name?*

Cathy: *Ohhhh, I get it. You're writing some type of juicy article or book on this whole incident, aren't you?*

Me: *Perhaps.*

Cathy: *Promise you will quote me as a resource. I would LOVE to see my name in print! All those snobby ladies at the book club would be so jealous!*

Me: *You're in a book club?*

Cathy: *Well, not for the books, of course, but it is a great place to get the latest dirt around town. You would be surprised at the things I hear.*

Me: *Wow, I'm sure. Well, I would definitely quote you as a source.*

Cathy: *A source, right. That's what I meant to say. Well, anyway, her name is Melissa. Melissa Atkinson. I don't know the name of the skank who attacked her though. But I heard those leather pants were HIDEOUS. She was not exactly a petite woman...I heard.*

Me: *Thanks, Cathy. YOU ROCK! And no, those pants were not flattering at all. Especially rolling around on the floor with Buncha Oats cereal everywhere! LOL*

Cathy: *LOL Well, let me know when the story is done so I can read it, okay? I have to run and put this last top coat on my toenails. Toodles!*

Me: *I will. Thanks again! Toodles!*

I plugged 'Melissa Atkinson' into Bing, *since Google was off limits*, and voila! Melissa and Sherman Atkinson's photo appeared. It was definitely the blazer/loafers lady from the market. They were apparently a well-to-do couple who donated quite a bit to charities around town. Sherman owns a successful marketing agency called The Atkinson Firm that has produced many successful print ads and jingles for popular television and radio commercials.

It looks like Melissa Atkinson is a housewife and mother to their nineteen-year-old son, Mark.

Based on this events calendar, there is a charity event tonight at the Glacier Hotel ballroom. Hmmmmmm. Perhaps I could get close enough to Mrs. Atkinson to get the inside scoop on the market catfight. If I could use this in my next book, it would surely be considered research.

Although the event was way past my bedtime, I voted 'yay' to a new adventure.

I clicked the link to purchase and print a ticket.

If I started getting ready now, I could make it just in time. Good thing there's a rental gown shop right down the street, which happens to be run by an old friend of mine. I thumbed through my Rolodex to find her number.

"Ava darrrrrlinnng, it's Anna!" I sang into the phone. "How fast can you have a gown ready for me? I've been invited to a charity ball."

It was going to be a fabulous night after all!

Chapter 7

Honey, I'm Hooooooome

John

Cruising home in my patrol car, I was feeling good, singing along to one of my favorite soft rock songs from the '80s, *Cool Night* by Paul Davis.

For the first time in a long time, I caught a break on the night shift. One of the guys who called in sick from the 5am shift was feeling better and offered to take over. He said he was, "already up anyway, so what the heck". He heard I had shortened my date with Anna to work a double and felt terrible.

I couldn't wait to snuggle on the couch next to my rosebud and watch Letterman.

As my hip vibrated, I thought it was Anna reading my mind again and checking in. I couldn't wait to tell her I was almost home. But when I looked at the screen, it was my brother's number. He always was a night owl.

"Scott, what's shakin'?" was how I always answered his calls.

"Nothing much, Bro. Did I catch you at a bad time?"

"Just heading home from a double. About to catch some z's."

"And not alone, so I heard from Mom and Dad," he said jokingly.

"So they told you about Anna?" I rolled my eyes. "It's really no big deal."

"No big deal? I disagree, Bro. I mean, Martha was great, and I respect your loyalty; but it was time you moved on. A man has needs, you know?"

His voice was getting louder. I was wondering if he had been drinking again. Definitely a violation of his probation, but that had never stopped him before. With only one year left, I wondered if he would screw it up again somehow.

"I get it, Scott. You doin' okay?" I asked with apprehension.

"Who me? I'm cool as a cucumber, Bro. Got me a new job, a new lady, a new place to crash outside of that pain-in-the-ass halfway house. I'm good."

"Well, I hope you stay 'cool as a cucumber' and out of trouble. Mom, Dad, and I are all rooting for you, okay? We love you."

"Enough with all the mushy stuff, Bro, I'm cool. Just called to tell you I'm glad you're finally moving on with a new chick, and I hope I can visit soon. Okay?" he asked.

That was the last thing I needed in my life. But I responded, "Sure Scott. Talk soon." I disconnected the call.

Both of us started out rocky, often getting into trouble as teens and young adults. However, it's ironic how one of us ended up behind bars for breaking the law, and the other outside the bars, as an officer of the law.

They say if a man doesn't have it together by his forties, there's no chance for him. I hope that's not true, because Scott is a smart guy; he's just impulsive and lacks direction.

I pulled up to the house, and it was already dark inside. Maybe Anna went to bed early.

I can tell she knows me very well because she left a note on top of the tray of biscotti. *Dinner plate in fridge. Be back later, had to run a quick errand.*

Who runs an errand at ten o'clock at night?

Further inspection of the bedroom and bathroom told me that she had showered, shampooed, blow-dried her hair, and sprayed on her favorite perfume.

That only led me to one conclusion. Anna was playing detective again, even after I *specifically* told her to stay put and stay out of the investigation.

Now I had to do some snooping of my own. I headed over to Anna's laptop and pulled up Google…checked the history…nothing. Hmmmmmm.

Next, I clicked on the icon for Firefox and did the same…nothing.

There was one more browser I hadn't checked, Bing. I pulled it up…Bingo! No pun intended.

How she managed to find this woman's name was beyond me, but she did. She was reviewing a *Who's Who?* page of the rich and famous featuring Melissa and Sherman Atkinson. It talks about their company, their charities, their family life. Geez! Anna probably knows more about them than I do!

I jumped over to the History tab to see what else Anna had found. Looks like a purchase receipt for a ticket to an event. An event that just happens to be hosted by The Atkinson Firm! You have got to be kidding me!

For the life of me, I cannot figure out why she would want to talk to this poor lady. Or what her reasoning was for wanting to go to this event.

If I leave now, I may be able to make it there in time. I won't meet the dress code standards, but I can at least get my girlfriend/detective out of there in time to save everyone from any embarrassment.

I plugged the address into the GPS for the Glacier Hotel and took a deep breath. So much for a quiet night.

Chapter 8

Step-2-3, Step-2-3, Gotcha!

Anna

I pulled up to the Glacier Hotel, and already my feet were killing me. I despise heels. If it were socially and fashionably accepted, I would be in flats with my gown.

I zoomed past the valet parking driveway and followed the signs for visitor parking around the back of the hotel. I managed to find a spot, but it was considerably far from the entrance. Just the thought of the long walk was making my feet throb even more. Ugh!

However, it was a beautiful building of, what looked like, twenty floors of rooms with oversized balconies. I could see some of the rich and famous lounging and yapping on their cell phones — probably about closing some big deal or inviting friends to come party with them on their yacht. Ha!

I grabbed my ticket off the seat and headed for the entrance in my best runway walk, without tripping on the concrete in my only pair of fancy heels.

A large waterfall was out front displaying various colored lights, while elevator music played softly in the background.

As I walked in, a man in a hotel uniform took my ticket and pointed me towards the ballroom doors.

I opened the door, and my ears were immediately flooded with big band music. Loud, but nice. I never learned how to ballroom dance or waltz, but I remember sitting outside the theatre at my high school one day after school waiting for my ride home, hearing "one-two-three, step-two-three, one-two-three, step-two-three." I had assumed that someone was learning how to dance and that the tempo matched a ballroom theme.

Entranced in the music by the band in the front of the room, I almost lost my footing as a tray of hors d'oeuvres flew past me. By the time I called out to get their attention, they were gone.

I managed to snag another server with a tray of champagne. I had no intention of drinking but wanted to have something in my hand, so I didn't feel as awkward standing alone donning a fake smile.

I slowly sauntered to the mingling area of the room that looked to be set aside for women and looked for Melissa Atkinson. I was trying to appear casual, engaging in a conversation with a thin brunette, who was evidently proud of her plastic surgeon's enhancement skills as she thrust her shoulders back, when someone tapped me on the shoulder. The busty brunette wrinkled her nose and sucked her teeth, apparently upset she was being interrupted in the middle of her debate about different teeth whitening procedures. As I turned, I was greeted by a handsome older gentleman in a tuxedo that was a bit too large for his feeble frame.

"May I have this dance?" he asked.

"Oh, I'm so sorry, I don't dance. I mean, I can't dance. I mean, I have a boyfriend. I'm sorry, will you excuse me?" I rambled like a bumbling buffoon.

I left the brunette and the older man to mingle amongst themselves as I headed for the buffet table. There were mountains of shrimp cocktail, shrimp puffs, scallop and bacon wraps, caviar, and a few items I didn't recognize.

I was adding some shrimp puffs to a small plate when I spotted Melissa Atkinson to the right of the buffet table.

I grabbed a napkin and side-stepped her way as casually as I could.

"Melissa, so nice to see you! Such a wonderful event!" I exclaimed with my fake smile still pasted on. This whole scene was so out-of-character for me, but I pressed on in the name of research.

"Do I know you?" she asked with a creased forehead.

"Probably not. I just happen to shop at the same market as you do and caught the horrific scene this morning. I'm Anna. Anna Romano. Are you okay?" I asked as I pointed to the Band-Aid on her arm.

"Yes, I'm fine. Thank you. Will you excuse me, Ms…?"

"Romano. Anna Romano. You may have heard of me? I'm referred to around town as the author-cat-lady." I laughed with a snort and regretted my words as soon as they came out of my mouth.

Her eyes got even wider as she said, "Ms. Romano, please excuse me, I must use the powder room," and abruptly walked away.

Damn! I messed that interview up for sure! I really have to practice my social skills.

Maybe I can apologize and try again when she comes out. I've never been one to take no for an answer!

The time seemed to tick by at a snail's pace, and patience has never been one of my virtues.

So…I followed her into the bathroom to try again.

I had never seen so much shiny gold in a loo in my entire life. Bright lights, mirrors, a lounge area with more seating than my living room, and counters full of lotions, spray bottles and jars of candy.

I came at a good time because it seemed as though the stalls were all empty in the front. I went down the row of stalls one by one looking for a pair of feet. As I approached the last stall, I stepped in something oily and dark and noticed the door was halfway open. I called out for Melissa, and when there was no response, I pushed the door inward, and that's when I saw the body.

It was Melissa Atkinson! And she wouldn't be talking to me or anyone else! She was dead!

A red stiletto was lodged into the back of her skull, and she was sprawled over the toilet, eyes wide open, as if she was still reeling from the shocking betrayal of such a heinous act.

Realizing what the oily dark substance was that I was stepping in, I hopped back bumping into the stall door behind me and screamed.

I knew I should have checked for a pulse, but my hands were shaking so bad, I couldn't steady myself even for a second. How ironic that at this moment I had to pee.

The large, bright room began to shrink in size as more and more people began to investigate the source of the scream and the scene of an apparent murder. Someone called 911 and checked Mrs. Atkinson for a pulse.

She was undoubtedly dead.

I just don't understand how this could have happened. I was right behind her. It had only taken ten minutes, at the most, for me to reach the bathroom.

The killer had to have been watching her and had this planned out very carefully.

This was NOT the fabulous night I had planned.

Chapter 9

Dude, Have You Seen My Girl?

John

I was fuming all the way to the hotel. I knew she meant well, but Anna playing detective could get her into hot water…again. How can I get through to her? Ignoring the valet guys, I pulled around to the back entrance that led to the ballroom and parked at the curb. I told the hotel rep at the door I was with event security for the night and he let me through while pointing to the ballroom doors.

The music from the band was loud, the lights were bright, and everyone was either mingling or dancing. As if on cue, everyone turned to look at me, still sporting my badge and gun, wondering if there was a security issue they didn't know about.

Since I was unable to dig into my dinner plate or the tray of biscotti on the kitchen counter, I couldn't resist the free hors d'oeuvres flying by my nose on those shiny, silver trays with their wafting aromas of seafood and bacon. I downed a few before going on the hunt for Anna.

"John, what are you doing here?" a voice said to me from behind.

I stopped mid-chew, turned slowly with my mouth full, and tried not to look guilty. It was the Police Commissioner. We had met several years ago at the Policeman's Ball for the Tri-State area. It was the last time I attended an event. Social gatherings are just not my thing.

"I didn't know you were into these types of shindigs, although I must say, you're a bit underdressed," he chuckled lightly.

"Just helping out with security sir. Um, actually, I was looking for my girlfriend, Anna Romano. Have you seen…?"

Aaaaaaaaaaaaaaaaiiiiiiiiiiiiiiiiiiiiiii!!!!!

I was interrupted by a loud scream coming from a hallway near the back of the room. A loud scream that sounded almost like the voice of my girlfriend.

Oh no.

Trouble follows this woman everywhere. I was nervous to see what this was about, certain it had something to do with Mrs. Atkinson.

I followed the crowd to the back of the ballroom and down the carpeted hallway that led to the ladies' restroom, conveniently located next to the service elevators. I made a mental note of this for later.

Pushing the crowd aside, I stepped into the restroom, slowly making my way down the row of stalls.

Chapter 10

Murder by Stiletto

John

Anna was leaning on the wall outside the stall being comforted by an older woman in a hotel uniform. The nametag read, Keysha Morgan, Manager. The first thing I did was flash my badge and introduce myself. Next, after making eye contact with Anna, I assured her everything was going to be fine and asked Miss Morgan to escort Anna out into the hallway until I assessed the scene. I also asked her to notify hotel security that no one was to enter or exit the ballroom until the police arrived to collect everyone's statement.

Miss Morgan took out her two-way and starting dispatching instructions to her security staff.

It was a gruesome scene. A stiletto…still stuck in the bloody skull of Mrs. Atkinson. However, it wasn't one of her own, as she was still wearing both shoes. She was slumped over the toilet sideways, facing the wall as if caught off-guard as she was entering the stall. Her neck was twisted slightly to the right, and her eyes were open and staring upward as if begging me to find her killer. I accepted the challenge.

Upon further investigation of the crime scene, I noted her dress was ripped and her hair a bit disheveled. Bobby pins that may have been holding her soft curls in a neatly tapered bun were scattered all over the floor.

Although the crime *seems* most indicative of a female perpetrator, I couldn't jump to conclusions just yet. I could hear the sarge's voice in my head saying, "Follow the evidence".

As I was texting Billings to send backup to the Glacier Hotel, Mr. Atkinson ran in, saw his wife's body and began screaming and sobbing.

I helped him out of the bathroom and had him take a seat on the bench opposite the elevators that were next to the restroom. As I waited for backup to arrive, I secured the scene, taking post outside the bathroom.

I would not let Anna out of my sight. She was seated across from Mr. Atkinson on another bench. I took out my notepad and figured I would start taking statements… beginning with Anna. Somehow, she had just gotten herself involved in the case, as a key witness, and possibly even a suspect.

Once CSU arrived, they would take her fingerprints to rule her out. Then we could move on to the more likely accused – the husband and the mistress.

I informed Mr. Atkinson I would be right back and headed over to Anna. "How are you feeling? Can I get you some water or anything?" I asked her, trying to remain professional in front of the onlookers.

"Yeah, I guess. I was just really cold, but Keysha was nice enough to get me this blanket. This is so horrible. Why would someone do something like this to her, John?" Anna's voice was trembling.

I didn't *want* to grill her on what she was doing here now, in the state she was in, but the conversation would have to occur sooner or later. It would have to be sooner. Otherwise, I may be accused of showing bias when the higher-ups reviewed my report.

"Are you up to giving your statement now? The sooner we can wrap that up, the sooner I can get a patrol car to give you a ride home." I was trying to encourage her to talk. I really didn't want her in the middle of what was going to become a circus. And I certainly didn't want her to be here when Sarge showed up. I was confident the commissioner had him on speed dial, and the sarge and lieutenant were already en route.

"I think so," she replied softly.

"Okay, Anna, so what was your purpose for being at the event?" I asked with my head down in my notebook, not wanting to make eye contact.

"I was hoping to get a statement from Mrs. Atkinson about the incident at the market. I wanted to make sure she was okay."

I nodded as I wrote, gesturing with my pen to continue, without looking up.

"I noticed the Band-Aid on her hand and tried to inquire casually, but she declined to comment and excused herself to the ladies' room."

"So, what did you do next?" I asked.

"Well, I, you know, I followed her, of course," Anna faltered.

"Of course. Then what?" I prodded her to continue.

"I found the ladies' room, and it was surprisingly empty. I remember thinking how shiny, bright, and gold it was. I walked down the row of stalls until I got to the one at the end where Mrs. Atkinson was slumped over with the shoe in her…oh, it was horrible. I just screamed," she said, as she cried softly.

"How long was it after your conversation before you found her body?"

"Well, I waited about five minutes before deciding to follow her. Then, I had to ask for directions, because I lost her after I turned down the back hallway. By the time I found the ladies' room, it had to be about ten or fifteen minutes later. She must have been walking really fast. I didn't mean to upset her, John, I really didn't."

"I understand. I'm sure Mrs. Atkinson just wanted to forget that whole incident from the market, you know? Put it behind her."

"I'm sure you're right. How could I have been so insensitive? Just to get an interview for a …anyway, nevermind."

"An interview for what, Anna?" I asked.

"Well, it's just that Cathy had mentioned it may be a good story for an article or book, and I thought…"

I cut her off. "Cathy Morton? Chatty Cathy Morton? You're taking writing advice from her now? Oh boy, Anna."

"I know, I know, it was a dumb idea." She was shaking her head with her hand on her forehead.

"We'll talk about that later. Just a few more questions. Did you see anyone leaving the bathroom when you were walking down the hallway or entering the bathroom?"

"No, no one. Just staff getting off the service elevator with some carts, but that's it."

"And when was the last time you saw Mr. Atkinson, if you can remember."

"Only when I first came in…by the bar. He was just doing some mingling, I guess. I got distracted by some shrimp puffs and didn't see him after that."

"Do you remember calling out her name when you entered the bathroom?"

"No, I don't think so, no wait, maybe I did. I'm so confused. I just remember looking under each stall for feet, to see if she was in there. And then I found her."

"Last question, Anna. When you made the discovery, did you disturb the body in ANY way?" I asked firmly.

"No, of course not, no! I accidentally stepped in some of the blood, but then I stepped back and screamed. I think you know the rest. Can I go home now, John?"

I had gotten enough information for now. And I made sure my phone recorder captured the interview, in case anyone accused me of being biased. Billings was walking up with CSU as I stood up to get Mr. Atkinson's statement. I met them halfway and pulled them to the side for a quick briefing.

"What do we have here, sir?" they asked simultaneously.

"Murder. Blunt force trauma to the head. The victim, Melissa Atkinson. And, um, Anna found the body."

"Anna? What was she doing here?" said Billings.

"Long story. But I have her statement already. No one was seen fleeing the scene. And I was about to talk to Mr. Atkinson about his alibi when you guys walked up. He's the guy in the tux over there, sobbing on the bench. He showed up about ten minutes after the body was found. He's pretty shaken up, but I'll get as much info as possible tonight and then get him down to the station for questioning tomorrow, if need be."

"Okay, sounds good. I'll be in the ballroom taking statements and getting everyone's contact info," Billings stated, turning to walk away.

As he did so, I called out to him, "Billings, one more thing. Can you arrange for a squad car to drive Anna home? Thanks."

Billings gave me the thumbs up and went on his way.

It was going to be a long night for everyone.

I ushered CSU into the bathroom to start processing until the coroner arrived, and then headed over to sit with Sherman Atkinson.

He sat up straight to attention when I sat down. "I'm sorry, I didn't mean to startle you, sir. Is now a good time to get your statement?"

"Sure, no problem. I…I… just can't believe she's gone, you know?"

"I know this is difficult. Nothing about murder is easy. I'll make this as quick as possible," I reassured him. Inside, however, I was giving him the side eye as I took his statement, wondering why it had taken him so long to get to the bathroom after he heard the scream.

He thanked me and agreed to answer any questions.

"You and your wife came to the event together?"

"Yes, we arrived around six to make sure everything was set up and running smoothly. My wife likes to…I mean liked to…handle the music and flower arrangements. I handled the food and beverage selections; overseeing the kitchen staff and preparations, including the buffet table," he responded numbly.

"And what time did the event begin?"

"Nine o'clock. But it didn't start getting packed until around ten."

"Okay, and where were you when you noticed something was wrong? You heard the screams, correct?"

"No, I did not. I'm not sure where I was. Someone ran up to me hysterical, telling me to come quick. That something was wrong with Melissa."

"You don't recall where you were?"

"No, I may have been in the storage area of the kitchen. My mind is just so jumbled right now, as you can imagine, Detective. I mean, what am I going to tell my son?" He began sobbing into his hands.

"I understand. I'm so sorry for your loss, sir; I just have one more question."

He looked up through teary, red eyes, and said, "Yes, what is it?"

"Can you think of anyone that may have wanted to harm your wife? Someone with a grudge? Maybe an angry employee or client? Anything you can offer would be helpful." He didn't know I was the officer who took his wife's statement at the market earlier that day. He also didn't realize that I knew he was a cheating bastard with a mistress.

"Are you kidding me? No, of course not. My wife was a wonderful person, loved by everyone. And she hasn't been involved in the firing and hiring at The Atkinson Firm for many years. She's a housewife and mother to our son. Whom I very much need to get home to, Detective…before he hears about his mother's death on the news!" He stood up and fumbled in his pocket for his valet ticket and cell phone.

"Thank you, sir, of course, you are free to go for now. However, we may be in touch in the near future for a more detailed statement," I said, as I stood to match his height.

"Very well, Detective. Just catch the SOB who killed my wife!" he spat angrily as he dashed for the doors to the parking lot.

That was a side I hadn't seen from Mr. Atkinson until now. I made a mental note and went to check on CSU.

They were gathering fingerprints from the stall doors, the toilet where the victim was found, and photographing and collecting the blood splatter to have tested. They also took scrapings from under the fingernails of the victim.

After taking the crime photos, the CSU techs were waiting on the coroner's arrival so he could remove the murder weapon from the skull. We were chatting amongst ourselves when Dr. Bernstein walked in.

"Morning guys and gals! How's everyone? I understand a murder victim deserves my attention," he said with his usual bellowing voice.

Either he was already up at home or working late in the morgue, happy for the diversion to get out and about. No one is this chipper at one in the morning.

"What's up, Doc?! Sorry to wake you so late, or early — whatever the case may be," I said, trying to match his level of energy. I pointed to the stall where Mrs. Atkinson lay.

"No sleep for the weary detective! I'm just happy to get out of the morgue for a bit," he answered. "Now, will someone please fill me in?"

"Female murder victim, the host of this event, with her husband. She came in here to use the facilities, but the perp had other plans. A stiletto was used as the murder weapon and does not belong to the victim. We wanted to wait for you to inspect the wound before removing it," I explained.

"Hmmmmm," he said, as he examined the injury. "I think I'd like to preserve the cranial area and remove the murder weapon once I get her on my table. We'll need to be very careful with the transport, to keep the shoe in place. Let's wrap the head in a separate plastic bag, just to be safe. I want to look for foreign fibers around and inside the wound, and we can have the lab test the shoe for prints."

"Sounds good, let's get her wrapped up. Everyone has been here for hours, we're exhausted." I clapped my hands together twice and chanted the usual phrase I learned from the sarge, "Chop chop, people!"

I headed to the ballroom to see how Billings and the other officers were doing with statements. The room was almost empty, so I assumed they were almost done.

"Billings, we almost ready to wrap up here?" I asked him.

"Yes, sir! Only a few more patrons to go. The only folks we missed were the catering team, including the bartender. They packed up and left before we could catch them," he said.

"No worries, it's late, and I'm sure the hotel would like to clean up and shut down this area for the night. I can't imagine what the publicity of a murder is going to do for this business. I know I wouldn't want to stay at a place that is known for murders."

"Not unless it was a murder mystery dinner theatre, sir!" Billings commented jokingly.

He could tell by my straight face that I was not in the mood for jokes.

"Anyway, sir, you will be happy to know Anna got home safe. You headed to check on her now?" Billings asked.

"Yep, Doc is finishing up with the body, and I retrieved all of the witness statements from everyone in the hallway who rushed to the scene when they heard Anna screaming, including Mr. Atkinson."

"What's his story?"

"Didn't hear anything, didn't see anything. Not sure where he was, but someone came and got him to tell him what happened."

"Humph, that's weird."

"Yeah, I told him not to leave town in so many words, and that we may need to speak to him further. Then, I let him go home so he could inform his son about his mother *before* he heard it on the news."

"Sounds good. See you at the station in the AM. Or *later* in the AM, I should say," Billings chuckled.

"Night, Billings. Thanks for your help." I threw a quick arm up goodbye, as I did a fast jog to the parking lot. I was desperate to check on Anna.

Chapter 11

Just a Quick Pit Stop

Anna

They tried to send me home in a squad car, but I dismissed the officer from *babysitting duty* when we got to the parking lot. I could manage driving home on my own.

I felt like a donut from the local all-night coffee shop was just what I needed to lift my spirits. A woman cannot live on shrimp puffs alone.

I pulled in, and there were a few police cars in the lot. I wondered if any of them knew John and felt nervous walking into the shop in a ballgown to place my order. I was supposed to be home recuperating from a murder.

I decided on a small coffee with cream and sugar and a chocolate éclair. It was huge, and I thought the cream and sugar in both the coffee and the donut would be enough to give me my second wind. I was usually in bed snoring by now.

I felt terrible about this whole situation. This poor woman was being cheated on by her husband, is attacked by her husband's mistress, and then murdered the same night.

I knew this had something to do with *leather pants*. And it was clear that the initials ML did not match Melissa Atkinson. Unless Melissa Atkinson not only knew about her husband's affairs, but also identified the initials of his latest mistress. If that were the case, using the mistress's initials instead of her own would throw anyone off her trail, making it impossible to trace the Dear Jesse letter she wrote back to her. And I think I knew just the person to give me the name that matches those initials. I picked up the phone to make the call.

"Hi, honey," I greeted John solemnly.

"Hey, I was just wrapping up a few things at the hotel. You okay?" John asked.

"Yeah. How are things going with the case?"

"We're in the early stages, so as well as can be expected. The coroner should have some results for us in a week, and I interviewed the husband briefly. He seems genuinely upset and just wanted to get home to his son."

"You think this could be the handiwork of the mistress, um Monica?...I think that was her name." I was guessing a random name, hoping John would correct me.

Bingo! He did.

"You mean Maggie? Maggie Levinworth? Who knows? We'll just have to follow the evidence as always. Just let me do my job, okay?" John asked politely.

"You're the boss! I'll see you at home." I disconnected quickly.

After performing a quick internet background check on my phone, I found her current address. Only a few miles from here. Great!

I wished I had time to go home and change, but John will be headed to the house soon, and it would be helpful if I were there and in bed resting when he arrived.

I thought about what Shirlene said to me about not messing this up and wondered if this was such a good idea after all.

I mean, who's going to answer their door at three in the morning to a total stranger?

I pulled up to the apartment complex within twenty minutes and headed to the door of 1A on the first floor. I went to knock, and I noticed the door was slightly ajar. The hair on the back of my neck stood up, and it was not instigated by a sugar or caffeine rush.

"Maggie…are you home?" I called out nervously.

Nothing seemed out of place in the living room or kitchen. I began moving down the hallway to the bedroom, still making casual conversation while breaking and entering. "Maggie? You here? It's Anna Romano, a local author. I know you don't know me, but I was wondering if you had a few minutes to talk, maybe grab a -."

That's when I saw the foot through the bedroom door.

It was Maggie Levinworth. AKA *leather pants*. Sprawled on the bed in red lingerie with a bullet to the head. For the second time tonight, I screamed. I grabbed my phone and called 911.

I had no choice but to wait for the cops to arrive. Neighbors were beginning to gather in the parking lot. John was not going to like this. Shirlene's warning echoed in my head again. I decided to text John and give him a heads up. Maybe it would soften the blow a little. I was about to press *Send* when I heard the sirens in the distance.

I waited for a response to my text while looking out the front window. That's when I saw the familiar car pull up.

John had arrived.

Chapter 12

Bodies Piling Up

John

I was headed to Anna's when I got the call. Dead body being reported not far from here: 1A Pine Run Apartments. I had to cover the scene since Billings was still at the hotel.

Then I received a text from Anna. Don't be mad. I'll explain when you get here.

I asked her where 'here' was and she responded Apt 1A.

She just doesn't know how to listen! THE MOST STUBBORN WOMAN ON EARTH!

I pulled up to the apartment and saw the lights to the front room on, and Anna's head in the front window, peeking through the blinds. I instructed the residents gathered out front to go back to their homes and stay inside.

When I walked in, Anna was sitting on the velvet couch biting her cuticles. Her head was down in shame, and she didn't even try to explain. I dove right in. "I thought I told you to go home and let me do my job! What are you doing at a suspect's home? And how did you even get her name and address?"

After I said it aloud, I realized how. It was me. I was the idiot who was tricked into saying her full name.

"Ahhhhhh, you tricked me. You knew the name of the mistress wasn't Monica. And I'm assuming the internet has something to do with you finding out her address?"

She nodded.

"Did you touch anything in the house?" I asked abruptly.

"The front door, the light switch, and the bedroom door. But I didn't know it was a crime scene! The front door was already open. I just wanted to talk to her. I was calling out her name when I saw her laying on the bed…SHOT TO DEATH!"

Anna was now on the sofa crying, for the second time in one night. I absolutely hate to see a woman cry.

"Well, it's a good thing we have your fingerprints on file already. But you know we'll have to test your hands for gunshot residue!"

"Okay, okay, just don't yell at me. I've had a rough night, you know?"

I lowered my head, sighed, and ran my hand over my face all at once.

"I know. You'll be okay, just don't cry. Tell me exactly what happened."

Anna was starting to ramble. "I just wanted cream and sugar, you know? I never wanted a bullet to the head! And if she would've just answered when I called out to her, but she didn't…and now we'll never be able to grab a coffee together!"

It was clear Anna was slowly losing it. I had no idea what she was talking about. I would have to get her formal statement later. For now, I just needed to test her hands. I had a kit in the car I could use, just to get her out of here and home.

It was looking like I was going to be working a double-triple shift. So much for a night off. After I was done testing her hands, I sent her home...again.

I told her to turn on the alarm when she arrived home, since we didn't know what we were dealing with yet, and I probably wouldn't be back for a while.

***

Billings walked into unit 1A, the second crime scene of the night, as Anna was leaving and did a double take.

"I thought Anna went home a while ago?" he asked, noticeably as confused as I was.

"Long story. She happened to be the one to find this body too, if you can believe it," I relayed to my partner.

"Oh boy. So who does this body belong to?" Billings asked.

"None other than the mistress of Sherman Atkinson."

"You've got to be kidding me?" he exclaimed while sighing aloud.

"I wish. And word just came down. Captain wants us working both cases since I handled the incident between our two victims at the market earlier."

CSU techs from the day shift walked in rolling their eyes.

"What's up with all the dead bodies piling up in one day, Solace? Night crew just finished with one of your cases over at the Glacier Hotel. You're keeping us busy, huh?" the older kid joked. His nametag read Victor. He looked like he was fresh out of forensics school. Pimply-faced, twenty-something, probably lived on caffeine, beer, random one-night stands, Domino's pizza, and Xbox Live.

His partner looked to be about thirty. A woman of no-nonsense character with thick bifocals, hair in a bun, and clear braces over her teeth. Her nametag read Carmen. She evidently didn't find the situation funny.

"Just trying to give you guys some job security. You should be thanking me!" I joked along with Victor, showing I was not as old as I looked and could hang with the best of them.

He didn't get the joke.

"Where's the DB, dude?" Victor asked grudgingly. Now all of a sudden he was down to business. Go figure.

I pointed to the back bedroom for them to start processing, while I put on a pair of latex gloves and began inspecting the other rooms. "Be sure and get pictures of everything, including the blood splatter on the wall and headboard. When you're done, we need to get prints from the front door, the bathroom, and these dishes on the kitchen table. Also, don't forget to check the sink and shower drains for blood," I yelled after them.

I nudged Billings towards the kitchen area. "Check out the set up on the table. Looks like she had some company."

There were two plates and two forks in the sink to suggest she had company earlier in the day or evening. The bottle of wine remained on the table with two wine glasses. Only one was still half-full.

"You think Sherman was here before the charity event?" he asked.

"I don't know, maybe. We're *certainly* going to have to bring Mr. Atkinson in for a more thorough questioning now. It is not looking good for Mr. Popularity."

"Talking about me behind my back again, Detective?" a voice bellowed from behind me. It was Doc Bernstein.

"Nope! We were talking about our main suspect, Sherman Atkinson. He's now being considered in *both* murders tonight," I retorted.

"Well, he certainly gets around, if you know what I mean," Bernstein laughed, as boisterous as usual.

"Indeed he does, Doc. Your body is right down that hallway, in the bedroom." I raised my hand to point him in the right direction.

He put his hand up to stop me. "No need for the grand tour, Detective! I'll just follow the smell of decomp!" He began laughing again.

I swear I have to find out what coffee blend this guy drinks.

Billings and I looked at each other, as if thinking the same thing, and headed to the car for a quick coffee break.

It was six in the morning, and the residents of the Pine Run apartment complex should be rising and shining, and hopefully ready to answer some questions. We were prepared to hear about anything they might have seen or heard in the past twenty-four hours. Of course, after numerous inquiries, it was determined no one heard or saw anything.

After a few hours, CSU had finished processing the scene, and we had taken statements from everyone. Doc had already left with the body, and we all met up in the parking lot for a quick debrief.

"So, what do you have for me, Carmen? Just an initial assessment, of course. No pressure." I tried to sound as non-threatening in my tone as possible, but honestly, I was in a rush to go home and sleep.

"Sure, no problem, Detective Solace. There were no signs of forced entry at the front door, so perhaps she knew her assailant. The cause of death is homicide, close-range shot to the forehead by a 22-caliber weapon, not found in the apartment. The victim may have been resting at the time or possibly drugged since there were no defensive wounds. There was blood found in the sink, but not the shower, so maybe the assailant washed his hands before he left. I also found seminal fluids on the bed sheet, possibly two contributions. We'll know more about DNA profiles in a few weeks. Fingerprints will be logged and checked against CODIS later today, and any fibers found will be sent to trace," she summarized.

"How soon before we get the tox screen back?" I asked.

"A few days," she answered stoically. She would be a great poker player. No one would know if she was bluffing or not.

"Okay, thanks. Let us know when you have anything to share."

Billings turned to me and said, "Time to catch some z's sir?"

"For sure, Billings, for sure. Let's meet back at the station at four this afternoon. I already set up the interview with Sherman. Sarge sent me a message a while ago to let me know he lawyered up. They're both meeting us there for the interrogation…I mean, questioning."

"Sounds good, sir."

I was playing *You Belong to Me* by the Doobie Brothers on my mp3 all the way home. No matter what this woman gets herself into, she'll always be my rosebud.

Somebody Get Me an Aspirin

Anna

Itexted Shirlene before I started my drive home, hoping she was up or at least had her phone on vibrate if she was asleep.

I began driving, replaying the past twenty-four hours in my head. Two bodies in one night is a record, even for me. Chatty Cathy got me all worked up about a hot, new story. I should have just listened to John and stayed out of it.

Now, all I want to do is take a pain pill for the hammering going on in my head and relax.

I was turning onto my street when my cell rang.

"Okay, spit it out. What'd you do this time?" Shirlene asked in a huff.

"Well, it's hard to put into words…um…" I stuttered. The Booker had that effect on me. She was almost always right. Okay, she was always right.

"Just spit it out, Anna," she persisted.

"I may have stumbled across a body…or two" I mumbled.

"You what? Are you saying you came across two dead bodies since I last spoke to you? How is that even possible?" she exclaimed.

"It's not my fault. I just happened to be in the wrong place at the wrong time."

"That seems to happen to you quite often, doesn't it? I'm sure John is about to blow a gasket! Are you intentionally trying to ruin things with him, Anna? I mean, really?" she asked.

"No, of course not, I really like John. A lot. The first body was at a charity event where Mrs. Atkinson was killed, and the second body was at the apartment of Mr. Atkinson's mistress."

"Exactly what were you doing at the apartment of Mr. Atkinson's mistress?"

"It's a long story. But the point is, none of this is my fault."

"Then who's fault is it, Anna?"

"Chatty Cathy! She put this whole idea into my head after we talked about that fight between Mrs. Atkinson and 'leather pants' in the market yesterday," I explained.

"Who the hell is 'leather pants'?"

"The mistress, of course. Aren't you paying attention?"

Shirlene sighed deeply and said, "Either I am half-asleep, or your adventures are getting even more bizarre. How about this? You go home like John told you to, get some rest, and for Pete's sake, stay out of John's investigations and any further trouble. Goodnight Anna."

The line went dead.

I grabbed my purse and headed to the front door. Once inside, TaterTot, my Persian, was the only one waiting up for me. I scooped her up and buried my face in her fur regardless of my allergies. It was just the 'hug' I needed after the past twenty-four hours. I kissed her and rubbed her under the chin while she purred. It was less than sixty seconds later that I felt the tickle in the back of my throat. Now I would need a pain pill and an allergy pill. Ugh.

I put TaterTot down and headed to the kitchen to make sure the litter boxes could survive until later after I had some sleep, and that everyone had enough food and water.

I thought about what Shirlene was saying to me, reverberating very loudly in my head I might add, while taking a long, hot shower. She's right. I don't need this type of drama in my life, and I certainly do not want to push John away. I couldn't believe I was thinking this, but I actually do not care *who dunnit*. I'm an author. I write books about murders, not discover them. After the Frederick Talon case, I thought that was all in the past.

I stifled a few sneezes while I put on my favorite pjs, set the alarm, and cuddled up on the couch with my babies. I'm pretty sure I did those in the wrong order. I could hear John scolding me now, telling me how important it is to set the alarm as soon as I walk through the door.

No psycho lunged at me in the shower, so I considered myself lucky…for tonight. My favorite crime show was on, and I was curling up under my favorite blanket on the couch; multi-tasking while I played a few games of scrabble online. That's when I heard the ding from my email app on my laptop across the room on the desk…

I was shaking my head *no…no more* as my eyes closed, and I drifted off to sleep.

Chapter 14

Interrogation Room #4

John

Thank goodness I was able to catch some sleep. Anna was snoring on the couch when I got home. She was resting so peacefully, I didn't want to wake her, so I showered and tucked myself into the comfy queen-size bed and drifted off. Tiny was at my feet when I woke up, with his arms outstretched and his mouth slightly open. I had to admit, it was adorable.

Anna was up baking Italian strawberry muffins when I finally woke up at three in the afternoon. Just enough time to get to the station by four o'clock. I walked up behind her, wrapped my arms around her, and took in the intoxicating, floral scent of her hair. She didn't ask about the case, and I didn't offer any updates.

Instead, we drank coffee and ate our muffins, while she told me about the latest episode of her favorite cooking competition show. Apparently, one of the contestants dared to forget the sugar in their ice cream mixture *and* undercook their pastry dough in the final round.

I kissed her gently, told her to take it easy for the day, and I would see her soon.

***

I arrived at the station at a quarter to four and gave Billings, who was already at his desk, a wave. I dropped a Ziploc bag with a muffin on his desk and told him Anna sent her best.

He mumbled something about a lucky dog and bastard, shaking his head. I'm pretty sure I was the lucky dog he was referring to.

Sherman and his lawyer arrived about ten minutes past four. Billings and I were by the coffee machine, dividing the roles of good cop/bad cop when they walked in. News reporters barely let them get through the front door. The news had spread fast, and now the deaths of his wife and mistress were all over the local media outlets.

We approached them, greeted them with a "Thank you for coming in", and led them to Interrogation Room #4.

Billings took the lead.

"You seem to be in quite a pickle, Sherman. How do you explain your wife *and* your mistress, who argued publicly earlier yesterday, OVER YOU, dying on the same night?" he inquired sarcastically with his hands open in question.

"You don't have to answer that, Sherman," his lawyer smirked.

"No, no, I want to. I can't explain it. It is unspeakable that I have to bury my wife with our only son by my side," he spat frustratedly. "As far as the other woman, well, Maggie was a good friend, and I'm sorry about what happened to her, but I **didn't** kill her!"

"Friend? Come on, Mr. Atkinson. Really?" Billings laughed.

The lawyer put his hand up to object, but Sherman was already opening his mouth to speak. "Okay, okay, so I may be a lousy husband who cheated on his wife. But that doesn't make me a murderer!"

"Let me tell you what I think, Sherman. You knew about the altercation in the market earlier. You found out your mistress had been in your house and stole the bracelet. She threatened you, maybe even blackmailed you for money. You sneak out before the charity event to kill her, maybe grab a stiletto from her closet, and return just in time to slip into your tux. Your wife confronts you again about your infidelities, maybe makes a scene, threatens to take everything you own in a nasty divorce, and you kill her too! Isn't *that* what happened, Mr. Atkinson?" Billings was fuming. He was a quiet guy, but when it came to playing the bad cop, he could win an Oscar.

The lawyer stood up, demanding an apology, dictating Sherman should not address ANY of those ridiculous accusations.

My turn to jump in. I extended my hand towards the chair, offering the lawyer his seat again. Next, I turned to Billings.

"Billings, that is ENOUGH! Mr. Atkinson is innocent until proven guilty, and as far as I know, he has yet to be charged with a crime! Why don't you get some air, I'll finish the interview, okay?" I stood up and patted his shoulder, pretending to calm him down.

After Billings left, I turned to Sherman and said, "Sorry about that Sherman, may I call you Sherman?"

He nodded.

"I want to thank both of you for coming in. I'm going to need your complete honesty to find the truth of what happened to your wife and *friend*, Ms. Levinworth. Can you be honest with me Sherman?"

"Yes, of course."

"The first thing we need to do is confirm your alibi at the time of both deaths."

"I remembered after I arrived home this morning, I was in the kitchen yelling at the staff when someone came in to tell me something was wrong with Melissa and to come quick."

"Great. Who can we speak with to confirm this?"

Sherman provided the name of the catering service and his contact there. He had used them many times in the past for various events.

"Now, what about the afternoon before the event? Were you at Ms. Levinworth's apartment earlier that day? Maybe for a little *pre-dinner and dessert*? Before you answer, you should know we have a forensics team checking the DNA and fingerprints from her apartment as we speak."

Sherman sat up straight and looked me in the eye before he answered. His lawyer and I were listening intently. "Run all the forensics you want. I broke things off with Maggie months ago, but she refused to accept it. Melissa forgave me, and we were moving on with our lives. I hurt her badly with the womanizing, but I loved my wife. Again, I was a horrible husband, Detective Solace, but I am not a murderer."

I remained unaffected by his theatrics as I spoke. "Did you or did you not give Ms. Levinworth your wife's bracelet?"

"I did NOT. I would never do something so heartless and stupid. I don't know how that psycho, may she rest in peace, got that piece of jewelry from my home! When Melissa told me about her altercation in the market, I was furious. We were going to file charges against Maggie the next day for theft and assault!"

This time, the lawyer spoke. "I think we've cooperated enough for today. Mr. Atkinson really needs to get back home to his son. He is devastated about his mother."

"Sure, just one more question about your alibi on the day of the charity event. Where were you and who can substantiate your claims?" I asked.

"I was at the firm working until about two in the afternoon. I picked up my tux on the way home, had a late lunch with my family, and relaxed a bit by the pool before getting ready for the event. You can confirm this with my staff and my son."

"Oh, we will. Thank you again for coming in, and we'll be in touch soon," I said, as I shook both of their hands and escorted them out of the precinct.

I stood at the door for a moment, watching the news reporters shove microphones in Sherman and his attorney's face, as they raced to their awaiting limo at the curb.

Billings approached, "Let me guess. He denied it all?"

"Don't they always? Our job is to confirm the alibi; and if there are holes in it, hang the SOB."

After updating Billings on the details of the interview, I asked him to get me the phone records for this whole love triangle between Maggie, Melissa, and Sherman. In the meantime, I was going to be checking Sherman's alibis and looking into the financials of the Atkinsons and Maggie Levinworth. If we could break his alibi and come up with a motive, the DA would have no problem charging him.

There were so many questions running through my head. *Who did Ms. Levinworth have an intimate dinner with if it wasn't Sherman? Why would she be upset about Sherman not leaving his wife, if they were through for months? If Sherman really didn't give Ms. Levinworth the bracelet, how did she get access to their home? Did the Atkinsons have a prenup in place? What would Mrs. Atkinson have been entitled to in a divorce settlement?*

It was going to take some serious digging to untangle this mystery. Which means I was going to need another muffin and a coffee refill. My Anna helped me through these long days more than she knew with her keen baking skills. I hoped she was having a lovely, relaxing day. She deserved it.

Chapter 15

You've Got Mail!

Anna

I awoke from a deep sleep thinking of only one thing, a vague memory of a ding from my laptop before I drifted off.

I had to be on my best behavior from now on though. I certainly didn't want to worry John any more than I already had.

I decided to make him a special treat, brew some coffee, and put my best smile forward. I was trying my darndest to get out of the 'cat house,' so to speak.

After John left for work, I took my coffee and tablet to the couch and cuddled under a blanket with Bette and Tiny asleep on my stomach.

There were a few emails from the paper for my *Dear Jesse* column and one email about how Viagra could change my life. I was about to delete the latter email when one of the subject lines caught my eye. It read, 'It was a Killer Charity Ball to Die 4, wasn't it?' I tapped the message to read the contents:

> I need your advice. I was attending a charity ball tonight, and to my surprise, the wife of the man I used to date was killed. Is it wrong to feel happy? Happy that he is suffering like I was a year ago? Even after this incident, I feel like I still don't know how to move on.
>
> Signed, mad4murder

Oh no. You have got to be kidding me. Where did this guy get the energy? Is this yet another player in this sick love triangle? It seems she didn't know about the other mistress's death yet. Should I tell John or answer her back in my column?

I decided to do both, typing a response to *mad4murder* first for tomorrow evening's publication.

> *Dear mad4murder,*
>
> *I'm sorry to hear the cheating bastard strung you along too! I've heard he has had several affairs on his wife of <u>twenty years</u>. But to be pleased about an innocent woman's violent death is just heartless. If that makes you happy, then may I suggest some healthy 'talk therapy' with a professional? It's time to move on and let this man grieve. I'm sure there is plenty of other married fish in the sea for you to date, but after the experience you had with this guy, I wouldn't recommend it. Have a drink on me, and toast to the single life!*
>
> *Sincerely, Jesse, Speaker of the Hard Truth*

I tapped *Send* and then dialed John's number. It went straight to voicemail.

My case update would have to wait until he arrived home later tonight.

What's In A Nickname?

John

Anna was in bed asleep by the time I arrived home. I had stopped by my apartment earlier for a change of clothes for the week. I thought about staying, but decided against it, with everything that was going on with Anna and the two murder investigations.

Since we began dating, I'm here practically every day…and night. I only visit my apartment on the weekend to get more clothes. It's kind of an unspoken event, but I really moved in a month ago.

I quietly jumped in the shower before heading to bed. As the water ran down my face, I pondered the events of the day in my mind.

The captain gave everyone on the case a stern talking to about closing this case as quickly as possible. Something about not inciting public panic with a killer on the loose. Afterward, he pulled me aside and gave me a private speech about my impartiality on the case because of Anna. Then I was grilled on why I didn't have a neutral third party, i.e., another detective, take her statement at both scenes. I tried to remind the captain about the recorded statement on file, but he wasn't hearing it.

It took over an hour to convince him she was not a suspect and that there was absolutely no conflict of interest. I believe Sherman Atkinson was our man and that we were going to break his alibis and help the DA get a conviction.

I toweled off, stepped into some pajama bottoms, and slipped under the sheets. Feeling a chill, I pulled Anna's favorite daisy duvet over my shoulders. This woman was obsessed with flowers. Which reminds me of my nickname for her…my little rosebud. I started calling her that after I caught her tending to the rose bushes in the garden out front one day. She was dressed in overalls and a white tank, covered in dirt. It was smeared on her face and all over her clothes and legs. She wore gardening gloves, and her hair was tied in a bun at the top of her head, with a few strands falling loose here and there. The icing on the cake was this one lone bead of sweat at the tip of her cute little nose. It was the perfect nickname for the perfect moment that was captured in my memory forever like a Polaroid.

Anyway, my main concern now is making sure my cases don't interfere with our relationship. Anna can be so stubborn sometimes, and after the Talon case, I just don't want to lose her again.

I drifted off to sleep with rosebud in my arms and all the babies on the floor, at the foot of the bed, sleeping. All except Tiny, who was laying on my leg, stretched out and purring.

Life was good.

Chapter 17

The Case In Question

Anna

I opened my eyes to view the hunk of a man next to me. He was already awake, staring at me lovingly. I could get used to this.

"Morning. How's my handsome detective?" I asked.

"Feeling refreshed after some much-needed sleep."

"I must have been knocked out; I didn't even hear you come in."

"It's okay, rosebud. I didn't want to wake you. You look so peaceful when you're sleeping."

"You probably prefer me peaceful and sleeping, because then you know I am not getting into trouble," I said jokingly.

John laughed along, pretending he didn't agree. "Well, now that you mention it…"

"Haha, very funny. You know, it's not like you didn't know what you were getting into when you accepted my cannoli. You met me in the middle of a stalker/kidnapping case," I gently reminded him in my most sarcastic voice.

"You're right, I did accept your cannoli with open arms. However, I did not expect you to continuously attract dead bodies, adding additional murder cases to my workload. And what's this about Cathy encouraging you to gather material for a new book?" he asked, and then continued on, "Nevermind, I don't wanna know."

"Speaking of dead bodies, what's new with the case?" I asked. I was hoping to find an opening to tell him about the email from *mad4murder*.

"I'll be interviewing a few folks today about Sherman Atkinson's alibi during the time of the murder. He isn't talking much and seems to be sticking to his story that he was in the kitchen at the time of the murder. The coroner and the crime lab should have something for us soon. I'll know more when I go in this morning."

"And which murder are we referring to, where he was in the kitchen?" I inquired humorously.

"Yeah, right? I do have two open murders to solve. But I was referring to the charity event murder of Melissa Atkinson."

"Oh. I see. Well, that's enough murder talk for the morning. Who's hungry for breakfast?"

"Breakfast sounds great. I'm starved."

"Okey-doke! I'll whip up some eggs, bacon, and hash browns before you go!" I replied, as I threw off the duvet and started to jump up out of bed.

But, before I could put on my slippers, John had grabbed me by the arm and pulled me back down onto the bed.

"Well, actually, I'm not *that* hungry...," he whispered.

***

After our intimate session under the daisy duvet, I skipped out to the kitchen to start breakfast, with a bounce in my step, while John got ready for work.

I honestly could not remember a time when I was happier. Except for maybe one childhood memory of Christmas where I had both my mom and dad together for a night when they weren't ripping each other's heads off.

There was an awful blizzard that day and Dad couldn't take off for the holiday, so he decided to drop off my presents that morning. Birthdays and holidays were Dad's thing, and he never missed one. Mom was there for me in sickness and health, school plays, and other mandatory parental events.

Anyway, Dad's car got stuck in a snowdrift, and he had to wait hours for AAA to arrive and tow him out.

It was the best three hours of my life. We felt like a real family. We made cinnamon rolls, sat by the fire opening presents, and laughing about the little things in life. And for one brief moment, I saw my parents glance at each other as if remembering the love once felt between them when I was conceived.

But, just as quickly as the moment came, it passed. Dad was off to his other family, and Mom and I were left alone cleaning up the mess: sticky knives with vanilla icing, discarded wrapping paper, and red paper cups with the remnants of eggnog.

I was deep in thought while beating eggs when my email chirped.

I froze, suddenly feeling guilty about not telling John about *mad4murder*... yet.

I walked over to my laptop and clicked on the new message. It read:

> I toasted to both of them as you suggested and didn't feel any better. With him free to fornicate, cashing in on her policy, and not making amends to anyone, I'm still unsatisfied. I'm sorry, but that doesn't sit well with me...please forgive me for my sins.
>
> Signed, mad4murder

Oh no. This sounds like either a warning or a confession. Now I knew I had to tell John. Mr. Atkinson could be the one in danger now. Even though he was a suspect, he should at least be warned.

John strolled into the kitchen smelling like aftershave and smiling from ear-to-ear. I decided I would wait until his belly was at least half-full from breakfast to tell him.

He was taking a bite of toast when I ventured forward with my news.

"You would not believe the strange emails I get with my *Dear Jesse* column, hun. Like, just yesterday, I received a message from someone who had heard about Mrs. Atkinson's death in the news."

My head was down in my eggs, but I could feel John's eye's bearing down on me. I pressed on.

"Anyway, it's the funniest thing, she seems to have known Mr. Atkinson intimately, and seemed rather pleased at his current situation," I said lightheartedly, while my heart was beating out of my chest waiting for his response.

"Anna, you promised!" he shouted.

"Now John, she contacted me. I didn't interfere at all. I gave her advice, just like I would any other *Dear Jesse* reader."

"And what advice would that be, Anna?" He was no longer eating and had pushed his chair back from the table.

"All I said was to have a drink and forget about the cheating bastard."

"And that was the end of the interaction, right?"

"Well, not exactly. She contacted me again this morning."

"Just show me the message, Anna."

I brought the laptop over to the kitchen table and opened the message.

He was quietly reading the message trail and then looked up in his most serious face.

"Please forgive me for my sins. What the hell does that mean? For Christ's sake, we gotta get this guy some protection and find out who this *mad4murder* person is. How many women did this Atkinson guy have?" he asked rhetorically as he threw his napkin on the table and stood.

John was furious. It seems that not sharing from the beginning was considered *interfering* and *deceptive*. Who knew? I did try to call him, but it went to voicemail. That counts for something, right?

"Text me your passwords. I'm taking your laptop to our tech guy at the precinct to see if he can trace the emails. I just hope we can get to this person before they do something stupid. She seems hell-bent on getting revenge. I guess she's never heard the phrase *forgive and forget.*"

"I tried to tell her that in my response, but she apparently didn't listen. Grudges aren't healthy. You know, I heard somewhere that holding grudges can clog your arteries more than cannoli. Best to just let it go and move on, I always say." I was nodding and speaking while trying to take the focus off my own screw-up and back onto the case. "Can I get you a coffee to go, hun?"

"No thanks. I'll grab a latte on the way in this morning. What are your plans for the day?"

"Well, you're taking my laptop, so writing is out of the question. Maybe just some shopping or gardening."

"Sounds good. I'll call you later to check in."

He kissed me on the cheek and headed out the door.

I had just finished texting John my passwords when the phone rang.

"Morning, troublemaker! What are you up to?" Shirlene asked.

"Morning. Just over here drowning in more hot water. It's a wonder this man continues to put up with me."

"Yeah, it is. You better get in that kitchen and whip up something fabulous to get yourself out of the 'cat house', missy!" she said. "Before you tie on that apron though, I need to video chat about some upcoming events."

I explained the reason why John had my laptop and told her I had Skype on my tablet and could meet in an hour.

After a long sigh and something about me being hard-headed, she disconnected.

I fed my babies, showered, pinned my hair up in a bun, and applied just enough mascara and lip-gloss to make it look like I'd spent at least fifteen minutes on my appearance.

I propped my tablet up on the stand on top of my desk and sat down in the chair. I could have laid on the couch, but that position always made my face look distorted.

I connected right on time, so as not to upset the Booker and was pleased to see her smiling face.

After exchanging pleasantries, Shirlene got right down to business.

There was quite a list of upcoming Author Meet and Greets lined up for next month. And, it seems I was up for an award from a national author organization in the category of Best Murder Mystery Series.

I told her John would be pleased I would be busy for a while and would probably thank her for keeping me out of his cases.

She laughed, told me to *be careful*, and waved "Hasta Luega!" as she disconnected.

I waved back with the promise of having her over for dinner soon.

Chapter 18

Guilt By Elimination

John

With the Dear Jesse email out of her hands, Anna should be completely off-the-case. Tech was making progress with the trace, but still no word on a name and location. ISPs could be a pain when it came to releasing customer information, due to privacy laws and all the red tape.

I was deep in thought when I saw a hand waving in front of my face. It was Billings.

"Helloooooo. What, no muffins today?" he inquired.

"Not today," I responded somberly.

"You know, when you two have issues, my stomach suffers. It's not fair," Billings said.

"Yeah, me too. I couldn't even finish my five-star hotel breakfast this morning. It seems Anna was contacted by a potential suspect."

"A suspect for what and how?" he asked

"For the murder of Mrs. Atkinson and now they are threatening Mr. Atkinson. I'm assuming *they* is a *she*, and *she* was a mistress as well. I'm not sure if it was during the same time as Maggie Levinworth, but I hope to find out soon. Anna acquired the messages from this person through her *Dear Jesse* column; and now I have tech trying to pinpoint the location of the person who sent the emails."

"Oh boy. You contact Atkinson's lawyer yet about protection?" Billings asked.

"Yep. Already sent a car out to the Atkinson home."

"Anything I can help with?"

"Yeah, if you could see how the lab and coroner are doing on the test results and autopsy findings, that would be great.

Sometimes a personal visit can uncover at least a few details to keep the case moving. Or give the DA enough to file charges," I told him. "Give me a ring if you find out anything. I have to head out for some interviews with the catering staff about Sherman's alibi."

I made a quick call to make sure this morning was still a good time to swing by and speak to the staff. Apparently, everyone who was working the night of the charity event was at work today, prepping for a party tonight in East Rutherford.

I grabbed my keys and headed out.

The owner told me on the phone to park around back. There were several white vans backed up to the door with script writing on the side that read 'Elegant Events Catering' and a picture of a white-gloved hand holding a silver tray.

The back door was propped open, so I went inside. As I walked down the dark hallway, the aroma of seafood mixed with something chocolate turned my stomach slightly. The owner appeared out of nowhere from a doorway on the right.

"Can I help you?" the small, elderly man asked. I wasn't expecting such an older man, since I was under the impression catering requires a lot of muscle exertion and heavy lifting.

"Mr. Cavanaugh? I'm Detective Solace. We spoke on the phone," I responded.

"Ohhhhh, yes. I'm sorry. My memory is not what it used to be. Come on in," he gestured. "You wanted to interview the staff from the Atkinson's charity event, right?"

"Yes, thank you."

"Right this way, they're all in the kitchen. Big gala tonight! I tell ya, these rich folks keep us quite busy, you know? Must be nice, heh?" he chuckled.

He announced my presence and purpose for being there and instructed everyone to cooperate fully.

"I'll be in the front, so you can use my office for the interviews. Just holler if you need anything at all," Mr. Cavanaugh added.

I nodded and thanked him for his hospitality and told him I wouldn't be long. There were two cooks, and three servers, from the event in question, and I wanted to interview each person individually.

I decided to use my recorder to save me from writing hand cramps.

I started with the two cooks and the one server who were allegedly in the kitchen with Mr. Atkinson before the body of his wife was found.

They all confirm Mr. Atkinson was unequivocally in the kitchen screaming at Jerry, the server, and Carl, one of the cooks, about the service. They all agreed he was a bit obnoxious and demanded perfection in everything and from everyone who worked for him. Apparently, Jerry had spilled a drink on a guest, and another guest complained the shrimp toast appetizer was cold.

He was in the middle of his rant, threatening to fire the entire catering company when someone ran into the kitchen and told him there was an emergency and to come quick. They found out a short time later what had happened when Jerry rushed in, gave them the update, and suggested they pack up and leave for the night. They didn't see Mr. Atkinson after that.

Next, I wanted to interview the other two servers who were out on the floor.

I started with the bartender, Louis. A young, Casanova-type who reminded me of Tom Cruise in that movie *Cocktail*.

I started by asking him if he noticed any interactions between Mr. and Mrs. Atkinson that night and then asked him how much alcohol he had served either of them.

Louis responded while rubbing his goatee with his right hand, "As a matter of fact, now that you mention it, I did notice some tension in the love department with those two. Mr. Atkinson was a bit stressed out. Put back more than a few shots of whiskey, if you know what I mean. I don't know about the wife."

"Do you remember where Mr. Atkinson was when the screams rang out?" I asked.

"No, sorry. I didn't see him, but you know, everyone was panicking and running around so I could've missed him."

"Okay, thanks, Louis. Can you send Jerry in?"

He nodded and strutted out, still stroking his goatee. Not the most sanitary habit for a guy who makes drinks for a living.

Jerry was tapping on the door.

I invited him to come in and have a seat.

Jerry was the nervous type. He was thin, puny, and very timid. I don't know how he survived serving the rich and famous.

"So, Jerry, you were serving on the night in question?" I started.

"Yes, sir. I mean mister, um…detective, sir" he stuttered.

"You can relax, Jerry. You're not in any trouble. I just want to confirm that Mr. Atkinson was indeed in the kitchen with you when the screams started."

His hands were still shaking, despite my efforts to calm him down.

"Sure, sure. Okay. So, it was a mistake. I backed into the buffet table and accidentally spilled a drink on a guest. And then, I guess I took a tray that had been sitting for a while from the kitchen, and someone complained the shrimp toast appetizer was cold. The kitchen should have told me. I really didn't know. And now, I may lose my spot at those charity events that Mr. Atkinson books with us. It's all my fault if we lose the account! All my fault!" Jerry exclaimed.

I sighed and took a deep breath. "So, Mr. Atkinson was yelling about all of this when the panic in the ballroom began?" I asked, trying to redirect the line of questioning.

"Oh, I guess so. Is that what Mr. Atkinson said? I don't want to get anyone in trouble".

"Jerry, I'm asking you. Just tell the truth, okay?"

"Okay, so Mr. Atkinson was yelling, calling me incompetent, and threatening to close our account," he recalled. "Then I ran to the restroom to compose myself. I was…well, I was…my face was…I was extremely distraught".

"Okay, so when did you hear the screams?" I pushed for a straight answer.

"I was coming out of the bathroom when I heard the screams coming from the ladies' room."

"Is that located near the service elevators?"

"Yes, why?"

"Just asking. Did you see anyone coming out of the elevators or waiting by the elevators?"

"I don't think so. I can't say for sure."

"One more question. You suggested the staff clear out when you found out about the murder? Why is that?"

"I didn't think Mr. Cavanaugh would want us involved. Bad for business and all. Was that wrong of me? Oh dear, I'm in trouble, aren't I?" he said in an even more panicky voice.

"No, you're fine, thanks Jerry, you can go now."

He practically ran from the tiny office.

After all the interviews, I could conclude Sherman was in the kitchen when the murder occurred.

As far as Jerry, he may be guilty of being cowardly, but murder, I seriously doubt it.

My cell phone rang. It was the tech guy working on the laptop.

"Hey, John! Great news! The ISP just released the customer record for that email to the *Dear Jesse* column. Her name is Laurie Richards. She lives in Edison. I'll text you the address," he said.

"Thanks. Guess I'm going to meet yet another mistress of the popular Mr. Atkinson. Oh, the miracle of the blue pill," I responded.

I hung up to the sound of the tech guy laughing.

Chapter 19

Getting Into The Writing Groove

Anna

Since John had my laptop, I decided to take a trip to the library and use one of their computers.

I had my earphones in, listening to music on my phone, and my flash drive in a port, ready to save.

I checked my email, and there was just one message. Shirlene was antagonistically reminding me of a deadline for a new book by the end of the year, only four months away. I lied and told her I knew and that I had already started it last month. Indeed, I was starting it today…in roughly ten seconds.

I opened up the word processing program and began to type my title: A Killer Charity Ball to Die For.

And now for a killer summary teaser to keep Shirlene at bay for at least a few weeks:

> *Everyone was getting ready for the ball of the year. Whispers were circling about who was wearing what designer name, and how much the Vanderbilts were donating. The usual hype among the rich and famous.*
>
> *The hosts of the party were experiencing their own share of whispers, but not about the ball. It seems their marriage of twenty years was on the rocks. When Mr. Palenta wasn't running his empire, he was off getting his scepter waxed by yet another ambitious lady.*
>
> *Most of his ladies had visions of grandeur about being the next Mrs. Palenta and living in the lapse of luxury. Little did they know, their*

dreams would never be realized. They were merely pawns in a game of chance.

But, one day, one of these ladies found out this truth and decided to take matters into her own hands.

Mrs. Palenta would soon be found face down floating in the family pool, surrounded by what looked like crimson ribbons shimmering around her body.

Which mistress would have the blood of Mrs. Palenta on her hands?

Solving the case would be like playing a game of Clue. Was it mistress one, in the library, with a candlestick? Not quite. This murder took place in broad daylight, in a mansion full of staff and family.

Perhaps it was for money, or maybe this was an act of pure revenge? The detectives were on the case interviewing witnesses when the anonymous call that would break the case wide open came into the precinct...

Now that I had my summary in place, I could start building my theories on paper and outlining the chapters. John would be happy to know I was working and not interfering with his cases, as a victim or a suspect.

After a few hours, my stomach was growling, and my caffeine levels had dropped below the concentration mark. I saved my work and headed home. I had to start on the chicken cacciatore for tonight.

I was waving at my babies through the front window when I heard the purr of a motor behind me.

Mr. Craigly was on the sidewalk in his motor scooter, hover-chair thingy.

"Hey, Mr. Craigly! How are you?"

"Well, I'm here aren't I? I was out getting some air and thought I'd stop by. Been seeing that cop fella over here quite a bit. Sometimes even overnight. Wanted to make sure you didn't go and get yourself kidnapped again."

"I'm fine, Mr. Craigly. Detective Solace is actually my boyfriend now, and I have a feeling you'll be seeing a lot more of him if that's okay with you…and the neighborhood?"

"Oh, I see. Well, I guess you have a right to your life. Long as you don't get into anything wild, like those rowdy swinger parties. That, I won't tolerate, you know?"

I responded sarcastically, "Of course not, Mr. Craigly. I would never think of having wild, loud sex with strangers in the privacy of my own home." I continued, "Is there anything else I can do for you? I have a couple of strawberry muffins, and some leftover biscotti, stashed away if you want them?"

"Well, if it's not too much trouble."

"Give me one second, I'll be right back."

I ran inside the front door to the kitchen and grabbed a ziplock bag and the goodies from my secret hiding spot. "Here you go, Mr. Craigly. Enjoy! See you soon!" I waved goodbye and headed inside to start dinner.

He grabbed the bag, grunted something quickly, and rolled off down the walkway.

As I was dusting the chicken with flour, I was wondering if that would be me in twenty years…grumpy, critical, and all alone.

How long would this romance with John realistically last?

Chapter 20

Chasing Down Leads

John

I hadn't heard from Anna all day, so I assumed that was good news. No reports of her finding dead bodies is always a good sign.

My GPS was directing me to pull into the entrance of the Shady Pines trailer park. Laurie Richard's home was a small trailer in a clean, quiet community. I knocked on the door repeatedly, but no one answered. That's when I heard a noise from the back of the home. Oh no, not with my bad knees.

I took off around the side and caught a glimpse of long, blonde hair flying in the wind towards a blue Camry. By the time I got to the vehicle she had already started it up and was shifting into drive. Fishtailing out of the dirt driveway, I caught most of the thick, brown mud on my slacks. Damn. At least I got her plates. I got an APB out on the car right away.

After hanging up with dispatch, I grabbed a towel from my trunk and tried to clean off my shoes and slacks.

I figured I would swing by the Atkinson's house and try to catch Mark at home while I was waiting for a lead on the latest mistress.

Just my luck, Mark answers the door. When I asked if his father was around, he said he was at the funeral home making arrangements for his mother. Poor kid.

I opened the conversation with "I'm sorry for your loss, Mark. Is it possible I could ask you a few questions about the day of the charity event?"

He thanked me, but seemed taken aback, and continued to stand in the doorway.

I assumed he was not going to invite me inside, so I continued.

"Were you at the charity ball the night of the murder?"

"No, I was at home," he responded quickly.

I noticed his tone went from genuine and sad, to nervous and fumbling.

"Can anyone verify that?"

"Yeah, the servants can verify I never left the house that night. I was logged into an online live tournament with my *Blood, Guts & War* team."

Since the game was online and used video and chat features, the console could easily be checked by our tech team. But none of that would be necessary if the staff could confirm his alibi. I'd have Billings take care of it.

There was an awkward pause between us. I was debating whether or not to ask about his Dad's affairs, but I figured he was old enough.

"I'm sorry to have to ask this Mark, but were you aware of any of your dad's *extracurricular* activities with other women?"

Mark looked confused, shaking his head back and forth in disbelief. He said he had no idea.

I wanted to believe him but found it difficult since the argument in the market made both the town paper and local news. However, at this time, I had no reason to suspect Mark for anything. He was just a kid dealing with the loss of his mom, and whose dad was a suspect in her murder.

I thanked him for his time and walked back to the squad car. My walk turned into a jog when I heard the radio squawking. They had located Laurie Richards, impounded the Camry, and transported her to the station.

Time to interrogate!

* * *

I was sitting across from a slim, yet busty, middle-aged woman whose eyes showed she had a tough life and whose skin indicated she was a chain smoker. I could tell she had been a looker in her younger years. I could also tell she was a natural brunette underneath a full mane of blonde, stringy hair. Her expression was one of boredom and annoyance.

"Why did you have to run, Miss Richards? You messed up my favorite pair of shoes, you know?"

"I'm sorry. I panicked, okay? Can I go now?" she said during an eye roll.

"No, you may not. Do you want to know why I think you ran? Because you were afraid we had found out about your emails to the *Dear Jesse* column."

She remained silent and folded her arms across her chest.

I continued on. "We take threats very seriously, Miss Richards. Why don't you tell us about your relationship with Sherman Atkinson?"

She didn't ask for a lawyer or deny she sent the emails. I sat back in my chair and waited.

When she finally uncrossed her arms and leaned her elbows on the table, I knew she was ready to talk.

She explained how they met online, and dated for a year, seeing each other occasionally when he went out of town. I could hear her New York accent coming out, as she grew more comfortable.

"I was, like, his travel companion…flying from Jersey to Chicago, Ohio, Cali, you name it. We stayed at the finest hotels, and his wife never interfered, even though I think she knew he was foolin' around on her."

"When did you find out you weren't the only one?" I asked.

"When I saw the story about the fight in the market the other day. Although I had suspected something was goin' on a few weeks ago. He was acting stranger than normal," she said.

"And where were you the night his wife was murdered, Miss Richards?"

"I was nowhere near the Glacier Hotel, you can best believe!" she was yelling. "That night, I worked the late shift at the diner. Go ahead and call them, they'll tell ya!"

"Okay, we will, I just have one more question. What did you mean when you said, *'Please forgive me for my sins?'*"

"Nothing, I was just joking!" She was pleading with me when I put my hand up to silence her.

"Like I said, Miss Richards, we take threats very seriously. We'll be holding you here while we check your alibi and the DA determines what charges they want to file."

Little did she know, we would soon be checking her trailer as well.

I left the room during another one of her eye rolls and had one of our rookies get their feet wet by checking Miss Richard's alibi at the diner.

I headed to my desk to call the DA. Billings had updated their office earlier about the emails our tech guy found. Her assistant answered and said she had a message for me. The judge granted a warrant for Laurie Richard's car and home, and she was being charged with Terroristic Threats under N.J.S.A. 2C:12-3 and should be held over for arraignment in the morning. The judge had also issued a restraining order for Mr. Atkinson. Laurie Richard's could not go within a thousand feet of Mr. Atkinson, a member of his family, or home, without being arrested.

Wow, that was a third-degree crime. Apparently, the DA took threats seriously too.

I had already sent a car to sit on Sherman Atkinson's house, but I also needed to update him on the situation. I called his cell to inform him of the threat against his life. He did not take the news well and seemed embarrassed about me learning of yet another mistress. He also seemed annoyed about the officer posted outside of his house. However, he was happy to have the restraining order in place, stating he had always questioned Laurie's mental stability. What a jerk.

* * *

I picked up the warrant and grabbed a few officers to help me execute the search on Laurie Richard's trailer. CSU was already searching her car, which was currently residing in our lot.

I was taken aback at the condition of the trailer when I walked in. Ashtrays scattered about, filled with butts and ashes, and the random piece of gum stuck to the side. Furniture that was worn and tattered. Clothes that sparkled with sequins and sheer fabrics thrown about; and a kitchen counter crowded with take-out containers. The shower stall was a tiny box between the kitchen and the sleeping area. The smell of the small, contained home was an off-putting combination of strawberry-scented body wash and Kung Pao Chicken.

This didn't seem like the kind of place someone of Sherman's stature would visit. I could see why she became his travel companion. Not that it was any of my business, but it was hard to pinpoint what Sherman's *type* was, mostly because he seemed to date women of every class, hair color, height, weight, you name it. He really put Melissa Atkinson through the wringer. That poor woman.

"Sir, we got something." An officer gestured me over to the sleeping area.

"I found this next to the bed," Officer Putnam said, as she held up a sheet of lined yellow notebook paper.

I put on a pair of latex gloves and took it from her to read. It was a disturbing note, supposedly written to Sherman, which seemed to threaten several body parts if he did not get rid of his latest playmate. The note iterated that she was to be the only side chick in his life and that she did not tolerate betrayal.

I was about to tell her to bag-and-tag it when another officer held up a hunting knife from a kitchen drawer with a drop of red on the handle.

I told both of them to bag-and-tag it and get these potential pieces of evidence to the crime lab for testing. Specifically, we need to see if the blood on the knife matched the unidentified blood found at the wife's crime scene. Which would clear Sherman of at least one murder…I think. There were so many players in both crimes. I was having a hard time keeping them straight.

I was feeling a bit claustrophobic with the three of us crammed into the small trailer, so I stepped outside to make a few calls.

The rookie picked up on the first ring. Laurie Richard's alibi was that she was at work from three to eleven that night, and after closing, she helped with clean up until midnight. However, no one could swear she hadn't snuck out of the building on her break after the dinner rush. And, unfortunately, there are no security or surveillance cameras in or around the building.

Next, I called the impound lot to see if CSU was done with the search of Laurie's car. They confirmed they were done and the car was clean. Damn.

I headed back into the trailer to see what else may have been found. I noticed a reflective glint out the side of my eye as I stepped inside and it directed my eyes towards the top of a large cabinet in the living area. All the way at the top, pushed towards the back, was a small jewelry box with a mirror. A ballerina in a pink tutu was posed elegantly on a stick as if she was about to take off in a graceful leap.

I put my gloves back on and located a step stool in the kitchen. I situated the stool next to the cabinet and propped myself up, stretching my body, arms, and hands to get to the box. When I finally grabbed it and lowered myself down, I thought to myself how valuable this must be to Ms. Richards, to want to hide it so well.

There was a cluster of childhood memories in the form of wallet-size photos, earrings, and jingly bracelets, but there was one jewel that caught my eye. A pair of diamond earrings that matched the pattern on the tennis bracelet Maggie Levinworth was supposedly wearing during the altercation at the market, which we subsequently found in her apartment. I bagged the entire box and added it to the plastic crate of already-collected evidence to be delivered to the crime lab.

I needed to head back to the station and question Laurie Richards again.

* * *

"We just finished the search of your home, Laurie. Do you want to tell me where the earrings came from?"

She was silent, arms folded in front of her chest again.

"You can answer here or in court, but it would help your case to be as forthcoming as possible. Did you break into the Atkinson home and steal that jewelry? Or perhaps you were working in cahoots with Maggie to stick it to Sherman once and for all, for his betrayals?"

"What? No way, you are not going to try and pin another thing on my ass! I think I'll take that lawyer now."

Ms. Richards was officially non-cooperative and very angry. I went to fetch the phone so she could make her call.

I was really hoping the crime lab would have some results soon. I had more suspects than I could count, and the list of items submitted into evidence was growing.

Chapter 21

More Money, More Problems

Sherman

I was driving back from the funeral home deep in thought. It was the first moment of silence I'd had all week. Me, the infamous, untouchable, wealthy mogul, Sherman Atkinson, was in a situation he couldn't get out of.

It was hard to believe I was burying my wife and attending the funeral of one of my girlfriends in the same week. I should have skipped the latter; the paparazzi were like vultures. What the hell is going on with my life?

What's even more insane, is the police think I had something to do with both deaths. I can't help but feel my past lifestyle is coming back to haunt me. Somebody is obviously trying to set me up.

I know I was nowhere near that bathroom when Melissa was murdered, but the one thing I can't figure out is how Maggie got into our house to steal that jewelry. Either staff would be in the house when I'm at work or Mark would be home, and he certainly wouldn't have let a strange woman into the house.

I planned to talk to him when I got home.

I don't know how Maggie's family found out about our relationship, but they tried to blackmail money from me for funeral expenses. They threatened to go to the press with details about my affair. They had no idea the cat was already out of the bag and that the media had already moved onto bigger and better news. I told them I would try to help out, but my obligations lay with my wife and son right now.

Frankly, I'd rather they leave me out of Maggie's funeral affairs. I don't want to be involved.

Sometimes I wonder when everything went awry. Was it after our son was born? No, it couldn't be, Melissa and I were great during that time. I never looked at another woman. Until...

I think it was around the time Mark turned five. Melissa seemed to be bored with being a housewife: the entertaining at the house every weekend, the country club, and the big gala events. She was depressed most of the time, and I was busy building an empire.

Instead of helping her through it, I referred her to a shrink and encouraged her to medicate, so I could be elsewhere and forget.

There were so many. Women, that is. Sometimes Melissa and I would be at a benefit, and one of them would walk up to us, speaking as if nothing had previously occurred between us. It was only an hour earlier, in a dark utility closet, that I was saying her name over and over in ecstasy.

Melissa confronted me about a few, but most of the women were unbeknownst to her. I think I was beginning to spiral out of control, becoming addicted to the rush. Some might say all the money and power had gone to my head. Sex in jet planes, restaurants, the most exquisite hotels....and now, none of it means anything to me without the woman I love by my side. The police needed to redirect their focus off me and find out who really committed these horrible crimes.

I pulled into the driveway next to Mark's car and headed inside to talk to my son.

I had to admit, the guilt was weighing me down. I was dragging myself up the stairs slowly, dreading the conversation that would follow.

I could hear the faint sound of gunfire coming from his room. He was probably playing the latest release of his favorite war game, *Active Military Kills*. When the funeral was over, I would have to set aside time to talk with him about his future plans, or lack thereof. I knocked before turning the handle and stepping into the room.

Mark looked up at me and paused the game. "What's up, Dad? How did everything go?" he asked.

"Good son, very good. I just wanted to talk with you for a minute. We're all set for the service in two days. She'll be cremated, just as she wished. And cards will be sent out to all of her friends and family members."

"That's good. I just…you know…miss her," Mark struggled to find the right words.

"I know you do. I think about your mom every minute of the day. She was a wonderful woman, the best wife a man could ever ask for, and a great mother too."

"So why did you…," Mark countered, and then stopped mid-question.

"Why did I what?" I was confused, and it showed on my face.

"Nothing. What did you wanna talk about?" he faltered.

"Oh yes. The police turned up some jewelry that belonged to your mother, and the suspect said she stole it from your mother's jewelry box," I explained. "I told him that was not possible, because the house is always occupied by either staff, you, or myself, and no one would have let a stranger, *male or female*, inside the home."

"Of course not, that's crazy. Maybe you should check with the staff," Mark insisted.

"That's what I told him, but I just wanted to be sure. I sure will. Well, I'll let you get back to your game. Dinner later?"

"Sure Dad, sounds good."

I was pulling Mark's door closed when my cell phone rang. It was Detective Solace. It seems Laurie was under arrest for threatening my life. A temporary restraining order was being issued in the morning, and there was a patrol car parked out front for my safety.

I peeked out of the window, and sure enough, a police car was out front. The HOA was going to have me thrown out of the neighborhood with all of the police presence and negative publicity around my home.

What could possibly go wrong next? I'm being framed for two murders, my life was in danger, and the police are telling me to watch my back.

I guess it's true what they say…more money, more problems.

Chapter 22

Conflicting Forensics

John

Billings said Bernstein needed to speak with me directly about the forensic results on both murders.

Frankly, I think the Doc's humor is an acquired taste, and sometimes rubbed Billings the wrong way.

I dialed the morgue and waited. Dr. Bernstein picked up on the fourth ring.

"What's up, Doc? I hope you got something good for me?"

"Well, if it's isn't my favorite dick!" No pun intended!" Dr. Bernstein laughed heartily as if he was about to deliver presents down chimneys at midnight.

"Haha. What've you got? These murders are kicking my you-know-what, and I need to get something to the DA to help them build a solid case."

"Well, what can I say, perfection takes time, and you are the least patient person I know. Anyway, yes, the lab is done checking the DNA and fingerprints on the plates and wine glasses from Ms. Levinworth's apartment. I took the samples you gave me and compared them myself. You have DNA and fingerprints from both Ms. Levinworth and Mr. Atkinson. Looks like you were right about the husband."

"And the bullet?"

"Just your average 22 caliber. If you happen to confiscate a gun from any of the suspects, we can have ballistics try to match the striations."

"No such luck, Doc. What about the stiletto?"

"Just hold on there, Detective, there's one more thing on Ms. Levinworth's case. There was evidence of intercourse before she died. A spermicide was detected. Unfortunately, there was no semen present. He must have worn a condom. Sorry."

"Crap! Okay, so what about the stiletto?" I asked.

"Ahhh yes, the infamous stiletto murder weapon. Just a partial, but we were able to match that print to Mr. Atkinson as well."

"Mm-hmm," I murmured slowly.

"I thought you would be a bit more excited, Detective. This places him at both murder scenes. What's wrong?" Dr. Bernstein inquired.

"It's just that he has a solid alibi for his wife's murder," I said.

"He wouldn't be the first person to have lied to the police, John! You'll figure it out, champ…gotta run!" he declared loudly.

The line went dead.

Gee, thanks Doc. Oh well, I would have to find a way to break the alibi or find more evidence that tied him to the scene.

I dialed the DA's office and got the switchboard. "Yeah, put me through to the DA's office, please."

Priscilla 'The Shark' Stanley had been a prosecutor with the DA's office for the past twelve years. She had an 89% conviction rate, hence her nickname, and she really didn't like to lose. She was a native of New Jersey and came from what some refer to as 'old family money'. Her suit probably cost more than my car.

When she stepped into court, he exterior matched her demeanor…fierce. Her hair and makeup were flawless. She was pressed, polished, straight-faced, and ready for war.

She picked up the line and got straight to business.

"You better have something for me, Solace, my case is slowly dying," she commanded.

I relayed the forensic evidence to her just as Bernstein had told it to me.

After a sigh and moment of silence, she said, "It's a bit circumstantial, but I've won cases with less. You like Sherman Atkinson for the two murders?"

I was flattered she valued my opinion and replied, "Absolutely."

"Okay, the warrant will be at the front desk. Pick him up."

Two counts of premeditated first-degree murder…Sherman was in a bind with no way out.

I texted Billings and let him know the caliber of the gun and to assign a few officers to recheck Ms. Levinworth's apartment, Laurie's trailer, and Sherman's downtown office. I would check the Atkinson home for the gun when we executed the warrant.

Money or not, Sherman Atkinson was going down for murder.

Chapter 23

Being Neighborly Just Doesn't Pay

Anna

Ohn had been working so many hours of late, I'd barely seen him in two days. I had some free time on my hands and decided to take a pan of lasagna to the Atkinson family before the funeral.

It was the least I could do.

I wrapped the lasagna in my insulated food carry bag to keep it warm and headed for the car humming to myself.

I searched the internet for the Atkinson's address, plugged it into my GPS, and started on my way.

I was rehearsing what I was going to say to him when the GPS told me I had arrived at my destination. I pulled into the long driveway and stared up at the large two-story home in awe. I was gathering my bags in the front seat when Mark stepped out of the front door and headed towards my car.

I stepped out of the car to greet him, and he offered to help me with the bags.

"Oh no, I'm fine. Thank you. Just brought a little something to say how sorry I am about your mom. How are you holding up?"

"Okay, I guess. Just headed to a friend's house. My dad's inside. Thank you for the food, it smells great," he replied as he walked to his car and got inside. Such a polite young man, I thought to myself.

I waved as he pulled off and was startled to find Sherman Atkinson behind me when I turned around.

"Mr. Atkinson. How are you? I was just dropping off a pan of lasagna for you and your son for after the funeral tomorrow. I know cooking is the last thing on your mind when these things happen. I'm so sorry about your wife," I said while forcing an awkward smile.

"That's very nice of you…Ms. Romano, right? You were the one that discovered my wife's body in the bathroom at the charity ball," he seemed to confirm and question at the same time.

I nodded with empathy. "Yes, it was such a terrible thing that happened to her."

"Aren't you also that detective's girlfriend?" he asked, as we walked through the door and graciously took the pan out of my hands.

"Well, yes, but…yes, I am."

As we entered the foyer and walked towards the kitchen, I looked around at the beautiful designs. Marble floors, exquisite art, abstract sculptures… "Was your wife the decorator of the house?" I asked in awe. "It's so beautiful."

"Yes, it was one of her many hobbies. She enjoyed collecting antiques and visiting auctions quite a bit," he smiled to himself.

As he was taking the pan out of the carry bag, and placing it on the kitchen counter, his cell phone chirped. His informant at the DA's letting him know about the warrant for his arrest. Suddenly, his facial features changed and he turned to me with a furrowed brow. "Why don't you tell me the real reason you are here, Ms. Romano."

Just then, my phone chirped. It was a text from John.

John: *Hey. Where are you?*

Me: *Don't be mad at me…dropping off a pan of lasagna at Mr. Atkinson's house.*

John: *He's a suspect in the murders. GET OUT NOW!*

The next thing I knew, there was a butcher knife to my neck, my phone had been thrown to the floor, and I was duct taped to the kitchen chair.

I was gasping for air in a panic. One wrong move and I would be toast!

"Why did you have to come here? Whyyyyyy?" Sherman moaned, as if in pain. "Isn't it obvious someone is framing me? They were just harmless indiscretions, that's all. I didn't mean to hurt my wife. Surely you can see how crazy those women are? You can see that, right?" Sherman was sweating profusely and had tears streaming down his face. It was clear he was beginning to unravel at the seams.

"Yes, of course. It's obvious you are a good man, Sherman. A man who simply got led astray by loose women. It's not your fault."

"Yes, yes, exactly! One of those bitches is setting me up! They're angry at me for not leaving my wife to be with them! Or, maybe Maggie and Laurie were both in on it together…to frame me!"

"It's certainly possible."

"Yes, you see, it's possible! Tell your boyfriend, the detective, that! Help him see the truth! Can you do that for me?"

As if on cue, John called my cell phone. I looked down and saw his picture on my screen.

Sherman snatched it off the floor and pressed the answer button. He was screaming at me to tell John he was innocent and that he was being framed. Instead, I cried out, "John, he's got a knife!"

Sherman quickly disconnected the call and threw my phone across the room, crashing it into a dozen or so metal pieces. I knew I should have gotten the insurance protection plan. Damn!

"Why did you do that? You stupid lady!"

Now Sherman was pacing back and forth across the tiles, with the knife shaking in his hands. I didn't have asthma, but I sure felt like I needed an inhaler! When will this nightmare end? I really hoped John had the SWAT team outside.

Suddenly, the phone on the kitchen wall rang. Probably John or the hostage negotiator calling to calm him down or see what he wanted in return for my release. I'd watched this scene a million times on my favorite TV crime shows and interviewed enough professionals for my books, to know the drill.

Sherman gave me the stink eye and threatened to cut me if I tried anything.

He backed up to the wall and reached across his chest for the phone, all while stabbing the air in front of him, mouthing something unintelligible, and daring me to move. I guess in all the excitement, he forgot I was literally *attached* to the chair.

"Hello," Sherman said hesitantly.

"This is Detective John Solace. We know Anna Romano is in there with you Sherman. Let her go, and we can forget all about this little incident."

"Lies! All you do is LIE! You set me up for murder, and you want to put me in jail, away from the only family I have left. You're not even trying to listen to my side of the story!"

"Okay, Sherman. You're right. Why don't you tell me your side of the story?"

While Sherman told his *'I was framed by a mistress story'*, I was trying to wriggle my wrists out of the wad of duct tape.

I was staring straight ahead, as to not draw attention to my hands, watching Sherman on the other side of the kitchen screaming into the phone, his face turning as red as a beet.

That's when I saw the red dot on his leg.

Within seconds, the glass in the kitchen window shattered, Sherman's leg exploded in an arterial spray of blood, and he went down on the floor, screaming in pain.

It was only then that I exhaled.

It was over, thank God.

Being neighborly just doesn't pay, I thought, as I glanced at the cold lasagna on the kitchen counter, hoping it would not go to waste.

Not Dying...Just Yet

John

Billings was driving like a maniac down the highway. Before we left the station, he had called in SWAT to meet us at the Atkinson home. As we were headed to the property with the warrant, I decided to text Anna, make sure she was okay, and give her an update.

"Oh shit!" I gasped looking down at my phone.

Billings squinted his forehead and asked, "What now?"

I relayed the text message from Anna, and his response was the same as mine, "Oh shit!"

When we finally got to the property, SWAT was all set up. The hostage negotiator, Sonny Pachenko, was on-site. I immediately walked over to the team lead, introduced myself and Billings, and asked for an update.

They explained that a visual into the kitchen showed Anna tied to a chair and Sherman holding a weapon.

I thought to myself: *Oh God, this can't be happening. Not after I waited so long to find love again. I can't lose her! I just can't!*

I made my way over to the mobile unit where Sonny was holed up. He was holding a phone and about to begin the negotiations.

I yelled out, "Sonny, I need to talk to you…right away!"

"Kinda busy right now, John. Can it wait?" he responded.

"No, it's about the hostage…She's my girlfriend."

"No way! I had no idea. Is this your case?" Sonny asked.

"Yes, it's a double homicide, and we were about to execute the arrest and search warrant. Plus, I have a rapport with Sherman Atkinson so it might be better if I talk to him first," I insisted, trying to keep the panic out of my voice.

He thought about it for a second and then handed me the phone.

"Good luck, John."

The phone was ringing.

On the third ring, Sherman picked up and greeted me hesitantly. I knew I had to reaffirm his trust and keep him calm.

I identified myself, informed him we knew Anna was in there with him and requested he let her go. I may have mentioned something about making the whole incident go away, but we all knew that was part of the negotiation rhetoric and that it would never happen.

He called me a liar and became belligerent. I was afraid of what he might do to Anna. During his rant, I muted the line and signaled to Sonny to get the sniper ready to fire when he had a shot, but NOT to kill, just injure. Sherman Atkinson was NOT going to get off that easy.

I unmuted and then offered to listen to his side of the story so that we could straighten the whole thing out…and waited.

Five long, agonizing minutes went by before I heard the shot. Atkinson was down.

The sniper got him in the leg.

I dropped the phone and yelled to the team, "Move in!"

I rushed in hoping to find Anna unharmed. I don't know what I would do without this woman. I had fallen hard and fast, after so many years alone.

I was literally running down the hallway to the kitchen. I could see Anna sitting in the kitchen chair with her hands behind her back. I smiled a half smile to assure her everything was okay.

I cut the duct tape off her wrists and hugged her tight while the medics tended to Sherman's wound.

I was resisting the urge to run over to Sherman and take my anger out on his face. I stood my ground though. Anna was okay, and that was what mattered. But Sherman would pay in court and stand trial for these two murders. We were gonna nail this guy to the wall.

After hugging me for a few minutes, her face wet with tears, Anna finally spoke.

I pulled away slightly and wiped away her tears. "You just had to get in the middle of the case, didn't you?" We both laughed and walked outside to the ambulance.

"I was just trying to be neighborly, dear."

"Yeah, yeah, yeah. Well, I hope Atkinson's son appreciates your kindness. I had a taste for lasagna tonight too. Darn!"

The paramedic gave Anna the okay to leave the scene, and I told her I would write up her statement later.

Since she was okay to drive home, I sent her on her way so I could finish processing the scene. We still had a search of the premises to conduct.

As she was leaving, she rolled down her window and said, "By the way, hun, I'm going to need a new phone."

I chuckled, shook my head, and walked back towards the house. Sherman Atkinson's son, Mark, was pulling up right as they were putting his father in the back of the ambulance. He could see that he was handcuffed to the gurney.

How was I going to explain to this poor boy that he would be attending his mother's funeral alone?

Tucked In For The Night

Anna

Once I was out of John's field of vision, the tears began to flow. One after another in a flood of emotions I could not explain.

I swerved just a bit as I dug into my purse for tissues. A horn blaring to my right let me know I went too far into their lane, and I waved my hand apologetically.

I couldn't believe how close I came to getting hurt or even dying, today. Being a detective in my books and being a detective in real life, were two entirely different things. John was right.

I pulled up into the driveway looking forward to furry hugs from my babies when I saw a shadow in the rearview mirror.

I was startled and relieved at the same time

"There she is!" Shirlene exclaimed. "My God, how are you, sweetie?"

With the faucet of tears now turned back on, I got out of the car to fall into her arms. I let it all go for the first time in weeks, and it felt good.

After a few minutes, she broke the embrace. She looked me in the eyes with her arms extended and gripped my shoulders firmly, "Let's get you inside, my friend. How do a hot bath and some herbal tea sound?"

"Sounds wonderful," I uttered. "Just wonderful."

When I emerged from the bathroom in my daisy pjs, Shirlene was on the couch with Liza and Sonny, and my tea was on the coffee table waiting for me.

She had already fed the babies and was heating up some leftovers in the oven, in case I was hungry. She was a good friend.

I sat down next to her and smiled.

"You want to talk about it?" she asked.

"How did you find out?" I replied with another question.

"Honey, it was all over the news. I almost fell off my chair at work when I heard your name as the hostage! You gave me quite a scare. I thought we agreed you would leave the detective work to that handsome, officer-of-the-law boyfriend of yours?" she chided.

"Apparently, even dropping off a lasagna for a funeral reception is dangerous nowadays. Who knew?" I said jokingly, hoping to get out of being reprimanded just this once.

"You knew full well that man was a suspect. But that is neither here nor there. You're safe, unharmed, and you're giving up all this real-life detective work. I need my favorite author and best friend alive and kicking! Speaking of which, your next manuscript is due soon. How's it coming along?"

"It's coming along great. I even finished the summary today. That's going to be my main point of focus from now on. I promise," I declared, holding my hand up in the air as a solemn vow.

After Shirlene watched two episodes of my favorite crime show with me, I started to get sleepy. She kissed me on the forehead and let herself out, as I snored softly on the couch.

It was late evening before John made it home, fussing about the alarm not being set. I opened my eyes and smiled. As long as he was coming home to me, I didn't care what he was saying. I was lucky to have such an understanding man in my corner; however, I knew that everyone had their limits and I needed to work harder to stay out of trouble.

"I'm sorry to wake you, honey, but you know how I worry when you are home alone at night without the alarm set."

I nodded and apologized as he reached down to hug me.

"How are you feeling?"

"Much better," I responded softly, trying to adjust my eyes to the light from the television screen. "Shirlene drove all the way here when she heard the news on TV and took good care of me. She's a good friend."

"That's wonderful, honey. I'm so glad she was here. It took longer than I expected to process the crime scene and complete the search of the property. I'm sorry," John apologized.

"That's quite alright. Long hours come with the job, right? So, what happened anyway? The arrest came so quickly, I thought there wasn't any evidence against him?" I questioned.

"Well, that's not entirely true. Most of his staff have confirmed his alibi during the timeframe his wife was killed, but he certainly could have killed Maggie earlier that day. We have his DNA in her apartment, so that case is going to be open and shut. Unfortunately, we have yet to find the murder weapon…"

Before he could finish, his cell phone rang.

"What's up, Billings?"

It was a series of *uh-huhs, oh-nos,* and *okay*s before they disconnected.

"That didn't sound like good news."

"Nope. Forensics just came back. Laurie Richards is a match for the blood found in the restroom at the gala where Mrs. Atkinson was found. And she somehow found a way to get Sherman's fingerprint on the stiletto, because we found the matching shoe in her trailer. She must have snuck out of work, drove to the hotel, and followed Mrs. Atkinson into the bathroom. Maybe she thought if she told her about the affair, his wife would get mad and leave him. Then she could have

Sherman all to herself," he chuckled. "Anyway, the DA is amending the charges against Sherman to one count of premeditated first-degree murder. They're picking up Laurie as we speak. I have to be in court tomorrow for the arraignment."

"That's interesting. It makes you wonder what the reason for killing his mistress, or one of his mistresses, could be?" I wondered. "I mean, why ruin a good thing? Maggie wasn't stalking or threatening him, right?"

"I'm not sure. This whole love triangle, *or rhombus in this case*, is too complicated. I'll let the prosecutor figure it out. I just hope they can put him away for at least one murder."

"If he's the killer then yes, I agree, but there did seem to be something genuine about him when he was pleading his case earlier…I just can't put my finger on it."

Chapter 26

Trial by Jury vs. Fury

John

It had only been a little over a month since the murders, and the trial was already beginning. Everyone at the precinct, including myself, thought it was probably some sort of world record, but a speedy trial is what Sherman's lawyers pleaded for, and that's what they got. Sherman's first lawyer was fired early on in the process. Sherman was convinced he couldn't get a fair trial in this town because there were people in the community who never liked him or his womanizing, and believed he was capable of murder because of his *moral* choices. As soon as his change of venue motion was denied, Sherman fired his lawyer and hired a team of three barracudas from the firm of Bernhardt, Badgely, and Moskowitz.

Apparently, this new legal team was so sure of his innocence, they were confident he would be acquitted. During media interviews outside the courthouse, they also spoke of how anxious their client was to get home to his son and how he was wrongfully denied the opportunity to attend the funeral of his late wife; trying to create sympathy with the public.

I actually hadn't seen Mark in the lobby or anywhere in the seating behind the defendant. He wasn't at the arraignment either, and I wondered if he would show.

"All rise for the Honorable Judge Bailey!" the bailiff announced.

We all stood in harmony and sat in unison when the bailiff instructed us to.

I gave a gentle smile to Anna, who was sitting in the back row observing with her pen and notebook in hand, ready to take notes. Billings and I were up front behind the prosecution table, prepared to testify.

Jury selection had taken place the day before. All twelve of them were sitting up straight and alert, trying not to stare at the defendant as they listened to opening arguments.

The prosecutor painted a picture of a womanizing adulterer who thought his money could buy him out of every situation, no matter what evidence was stacked against him. In this case, DNA – which doesn't lie.

He described Sherman Atkinson as a cold, calculated man whose mistress just so happened to have killed his wife. He also argued that when Mr. Atkinson was backed into a corner, on the verge of losing his family and fortune, he took care of his mistress in a cold and calculating manner. And then, desperate to beat the charges, he continued his streak of violence with the kidnapping and attack upon Anna Romano, which ended in SWAT taking him down in his home. In closing, he urged the jury to see Sherman for what he really was and convict him of premeditated, first-degree murder.

I thought it was a pretty good argument until Atkinson's attorney stood up and began to pontificate. His name was Arthur Badgely. He was one of the top criminal attorneys in the country, dressed to a tee in his Armani suit and wingtip shoes.

> *"Ladies and gentlemen of the jury, let me tell you the story of a man in mourning. Yes, he may be a wealthy man, but he is also kind and giving. One could even say generous. He and his wife Melissa have been giving back to the community for almost two decades. In fact, they were hosting a charity event when someone followed his wife into the ladies' room and murdered her. A senseless and tragic death that Mr. Atkinson had no knowledge of*

beforehand, and that which he is <u>still</u> recovering from. Yes, Sherman Atkinson committed adultery. He is a normal man, with normal urges, who made some mistakes in his marriage. But we have to remember the facts of this case, and adultery should not be a determining factor in sending an innocent man to jail for the rest of his life, leaving his son orphaned and alone.

Was he having an affair with Maggie Levinworth? YES. Is that wrong? YES. Did his wife know of his affairs? YES. So what is the motive here, ladies and gentlemen? The prosecutor's argument that Ms. Levinworth was going to tell his wife and expose Mr. Atkinson's indiscretions does not make sense. There would be no need for him to panic and murder her.

So how did Mr. Atkinson's DNA get on the body and other items at the scene? It's simple. Someone planted his DNA and prints throughout Ms. Levinworth's home! Period! The DA's office first tried to pin the murder of his wife and his mistress on him, then amended the charges to one murder, after they found his wife's <u>real killer</u>! IT IS QUITE CLEAR THAT THEY HAVE BEEN FRAMING HIM ALL ALONG JUST TO CLOSE THIS CASE! I REQUEST THAT THIS <u>ENTIRE CASE</u> BE DISMISSED BASED ON UNETHICAL POLICE PRACTICES!"

The prosecutor jumped out of his seat and yelled, "Objection, Your Honor, this is ridiculous!"

There were mumblings and gasps coming from across the galley, including from myself. This attorney had some big *cojones*, and it was apparent Mr. Atkinson was not going down without a fight.

The judge was banging his gavel, "Order in the court!"

He directed the two attorneys to the bench and put his hand over the mic in front of him. "There will be no dismissal Mr. Badgely, and your opening statement is over. Unless you have proof of conspiracy, this line of defense is OUT! Understood? Now step back…BOTH of you!"

Badgely nodded, and both attorneys returned to their respective tables.

* * *

Billings and I were the first to take the stand. We testified about the murder of Mrs. Atkinson and Ms. Levinworth and the evidence we found at both crime scenes.

Next up, there was a combination of alleged past mistresses for the prosecution that took the stand to say what a despicable person Sherman Atkinson was. Then the defense called multiple character witnesses that stated how kind and generous Mr. Atkinson and his entire family had been to them, and how they would never have survived without their generosity.

The judge called a recess until the next morning, and we all dispersed single file to the lobby to discuss the day's events.

Of course, the attorneys were running for the cameras. This was the most excitement anyone in this small town had seen in decades.

Anna was a chatterbox the whole ride home, making up theories and suppositions about the case. I just smiled and shook my head. My girl was a true crime buff.

Chapter 27

The Villainous Verdict

Anna

I was excited to be in court again today. My next book was going to be another bestseller for sure!

My handsome detective is all done testifying, so he sat in the back next to me today. I like being able to share this part of our lives together, even if I was only involved in this case because I discovered the body. Thank goodness John was able to get me off the hook from testifying. My affidavit was all they needed, being as though I hadn't actually witnessed anything, *or anyone*, at either crime scene. And, Mr. Atkinson had confirmed my account of what happened in his home and pleaded guilty to kidnapping and assault one charges. Whew, what a relief!

I had my pen and notebook poised to begin writing.

The coroner, Dr. Bernstein, took the stand and was elaborating on the wounds the victim sustained when Mark Atkinson walked in. All of us were nearly whiplashed and shocked to see him this late in the day.

I had wondered where he was and if he would show. I thought about stopping in to check on him, but we all know how that turned out last time.

With all the whispers and murmuring, the judge banged his gavel and ordered quiet in the courtroom. Mark sat down quickly in the pew directly to the left, across from us. I gave him a smile, but he was solely focused on his father at the defense table. Poor kid. He was probably still in shock, and not used to seeing his father in such a helpless state. The father who was in charge all the time, at work and at home, and so well put-together and successful in business, was now a common criminal accused of murder.

As Dr. Lee, the forensic pathologist, approached the stand, I went back to taking notes feverishly for my next bestseller.

Her soft, timid demeanor was a stark difference from the loud and animated Dr. Bernstein. Based on what John has told me, Lee was a newbie at the lab, but quite good at what she does. However, she seemed terribly nervous for some reason.

The prosecution stood up confidently and approached Dr. Lee. After having her verify her credentials and current role in the forensic lab at the medical examiner's office, he began his line of questioning:

> *"Doctor, isn't it true that the prints and saliva found on the wine glass, as well as one of the contributions on the bed sheets, at the apartment of Maggie Levinworth, were a direct match to the defendant?!"*
>
> *Silence in the courtroom.*
>
> *"Dr. Lee, please answer the question."*
>
> *"Well, actually…"*
>
> *"Actually what? Dr. Lee, please answer the question."*
>
> *"Well, after further analysis, I've found the DNA on the sheets to be a familial match."*
>
> *"What exactly does that mean, Dr. Lee?"*
>
> *"It means it could have been a sibling or child of the defendant, with common alleles. I don't know how this happened, but it is possible the evidence was contaminated. I'm sorry…I'm so sorry." Dr. Lee was rocking back and forth in her chair sobbing uncontrollably while wringing her hands together.*

The prosecutor was dumbfounded. His mouth was agape as if confused about whether to continue questioning or just rest his case.

All the jaws in the galley dropped, including my own. Since Sherman was an only child, that could only mean one other possible suspect. But how can that be? He had never even met Maggie. Or had he?

Sherman's team rose to their feet and immediately asked for a mistrial based on the new evidence.

The judge was banging his gavel like he was a construction worker in a past life. He demanded counsel in his chambers immediately and dismissed the witness.

We were all scared to move and miss the finale, so we sat for almost an hour until they all emerged again.

The bailiff announced once again for everyone to rise and be seated.

I glanced over at Mark, and he was as frozen as an ice sculpture. I wondered if he was even breathing. For a moment, I was tempted to pull out my compact mirror and check.

When the judge, defendant, and attorneys all filed back into the courtroom, the judge called order and made his final ruling. "Because of this irrevocable, inexcusable miscarriage of justice, I am forced to dismiss the case against Sherman Atkinson without prejudice, and without the ability to recall in the future. Mr. Atkinson, I am sorry for any distress this whole matter has caused you or your family. Ladies and gentlemen of the jury, the court thanks you for your service. Court is adjourned."

An uproar erupted in the courtroom. Half of the room was confused, the other half elated. The judge was banging his gavel yet again with a fury. As the jury was exiting, there was a loud scream from the back of the galley. It was coming from Mark. He was apparently angry. His gaze seemed to be fixed on his father, and he was screaming, "Noooooooo! You can't! You're wrong about him! You can't do this!"

John tried to walk over and place his hand on his shoulder to calm him down, but he shrugged his arm away and continued to scream at the top of his lungs, as tears streamed down his face. "IT'S NOT FAIR! YOU KILLED MOM WITH YOUR INFIDELITIES, AND NOW YOU WALK FREE! IT WAS THE PERFECT PLAN, AND NOW YOU'VE RUINED THAT TOO!"

As soon as we all saw the shimmer of silver in Mark's hand, slowly rising from his pocket, we shrieked and hit the floor. The bailiff got to Mark just as he pulled out the gun and took a shot at his father. The bullet was a centimeter away from killing a member of Mr. Atkinson's legal team and several innocent bystanders. The court stenographer wasn't as lucky. The bullet grazed her arm before it plunged into the wall behind her.

It was a horrible ending to a promising day. Why would Sherman's own son hate him so much that he would want him dead? And what did he mean by the *perfect plan*?

Wow. After all of this excitement, I would have more than enough material for my novel.

Billings showed up when he heard the drama on the news and proceeded to handcuff Mark Atkinson while John held him down. Both Billings and John escorted him to the precinct for booking. It was their case, and I am sure they wanted first dibs at the interrogation.

Hopefully, John would call me later and tell me what Mark said. I'm dying to know the details!

The Ultimate Revenge

Sherman

I should be happy and relieved right now about the outcome of the trial, but I'm not.

I'm sitting at a hotel bar with a glass of Scotch wondering where I went wrong.

My tombstone should read, *Sherman Atkinson, failure as a father and a husband.*

My own son tried to kill me.

Where did he even get a gun?

They're charging him with the premeditated, first-degree murder of Maggie, conspiracy to commit murder on his mother, the attempted murder on myself, and the assault on the court stenographer. Apparently, he had helped Laurie get close to Melissa by giving her the itinerary for the night of the charity. The earrings were just a down payment for the job. He even paid off the bathroom attendant to get lost for an hour. And, he had promised Laurie even more money if I was convicted.

As far as Maggie was concerned, he found her number on the caller ID, seduced her, and attempted to frame me for the whole thing.

Establishing his alibi was simple since he was smart enough to know how to rig the online game to make it look like he was right in his room playing in the live tournament with his *Blood, Guts & War* team. All that technical knowledge gone to waste. He could have done great at a school like MIT…if only I had encouraged him more. Pushed him to get his life together and get an education.

Thank goodness someone from the offices of Bernhardt, Badgely, and Moskowitz agreed to represent him. Footing the bill is the least I could do for my son. I made sure they knew about his prior admissions to psychiatric facilities. He had been diagnosed with bipolar disorder and mild depression at the age of thirteen, but often went off his meds, claiming he 'felt fine' and was 'cured'.

Because of the mental health issues, it was easy for his defense attorney to claim 'not guilty by reason of insanity or mental defect', to get the death penalty off the table.

However, even that was a challenge, due to Mark's stubborn streak, which he seemingly gets from me. Mark refused to admit he had a problem and refused the plea entry.

In the end, the past medical reports and admissions were enough to get it submitted and approved by the judge, and have my own son declared mentally incompetent to stand trial.

Between the refusal of the plea and his bazaar rantings in the courtroom, the judge had no choice.

Am I glad my son will spend the rest of his life in a hospital? No. Am I happy he will not be executed? Of course. What father wouldn't be?

* * *

I remember the allocution in court that last day, it was as if I was listening to someone I didn't know. And yes, at times, his eyes portrayed an evil I had never seen in him before.

Was this an evil in me that I had passed down to my son? Is this payback for what I did to my wife?

I'll have the rest of my life to wonder.

My son stood before the judge in shackles and handcuffs, donning a gray county hospital pajama outfit and said:

> *The rage inside of me had been building for years, Your Honor. Tiny pills that were meant to restrain me like these shackles you have me in were swiped under my tongue until my mother left the room.*

Some days, I just needed to feel the fire burn inside me. It helped relieve the pain, just like a razor to my arm. Perfect lines slanted parallel like an airport parking lot. One the same as the other in unison, as the planes landed above them.

The first time I felt the rage was four years ago after school. I was fifteen years old, and I decided to stop by my dad's office to surprise him. It was me who got the surprise. When I walked in, his pants were down around his ankles with his associate bent over his desk. I quickly shut the door and ran from the office. We never spoke of the incident, and I never surprised him again.

The next time, I was seventeen. Mom was away at her sisters to help with her new baby. I got up in the middle of the night to use the bathroom and passed the upstairs window overlooking the patio. That's when I saw Dad and his latest fling in the pool…they were not swimming.

After that, Dad and I didn't speak much. As long as I pretended he was a good father and husband, didn't tell mom, and smiled at public functions, I kept getting my allowance for whatever I needed and wanted. Most of the time it was alcohol, specifically vodka, and sometimes it was weed. I was no longer interested in college, and the sadness poured over me like hot sauce for the fury.

I not only hated him for the pain he had caused my mom, but I hated my mom for staying and not saying anything about the affairs, or even standing up for herself. Every day I wanted out of my dysfunctional family. I longed to kill them both but wanted my dad to suffer most. It was so easy to convince that bitch Laurie Richards that my dad would be with her if his wife were out of the picture. She fell for it hook, line, and sinker. [hysterical laughter]

And Maggie was easier to seduce than I thought she would be. I guess my dad wasn't as much of a Casanova as he thought. She was an animal in the sack. Obviously deprived.

Once I drugged her wine, she went to the bedroom to lie down. That's when I swapped one of the glasses for one from home with my Dad's prints on it. Afterwards, I went into the bedroom, shot her, and grabbed the shoes.

[turning to look at his father] I thought you being in prison would be the perfect finale to my master plan, but even that failed. You had to die for your sins, dear Daddy. Til death do us part. [more laughter]

After his speech and the uncontrollable laughter at the end, they escorted him out of the courtroom. The judge rendered her sentencing recommendation. Life without parole in an assigned psychiatric facility.

I remembered the hairs on the back of my neck standing on end, as I sat there until the courtroom was cleared.

How would I start over without my family?

And what was the point anyway?

Just Desserts

Anna

was all smiles and glowing. John and I were having our weekly date night. Even though he loved my cooking, he wanted to treat me to a fancy restaurant after all the excitement of the past month.

It was a beautiful seafood restaurant on the waters of the Atlantic. Although it was an hour's drive to Ocean City, it was worth it on cool, breezy nights like this, with the salt smell of the ocean blowing through the windows. Michael McDonald crooned on the radio while we sang along in perfect harmony.

We only spoke briefly of the Sherman Atkinson case and how he was recovering. After burying his wife, he immersed himself into the ad agency, opening two new offices in New York and Pennsylvania, and hasn't spoken to his son Mark since he was sentenced.

"I hope Mark gets the treatment he needs to heal; and I hope they both find a way to forgive each other and move on," I said to John.

Two murder cases in the small town of Princeton were solved, and the world was a better place because of my handsome detective.

I asked for John's insight on my new novel, and he redirected the conversation to how good the lobster was with melted butter.

I nodded and smiled, but I was still wrestling with a bestselling title in my head. Since the moral of this sad story of betrayal and revenge is *Happy Wife, Happy Life*, I may use that cliché in the title.

I was pretending to listen to John ramble on about how lobster traps worked, and glanced down at my hand and smiled. Maybe one day I'd find out what that feels like...being a wife.

* * *

Little did both of them know, they were sharing the same daydream.

I was talking lobster, but I was really thinking about the life I could have with Anna at my side as my wife — if I could manage to keep her out of the cases I worked.

I smiled to myself and thought Martha would be happy for me. Happy that I chose to move on instead of wallowing in sadness and despair for the rest of my life, never letting anyone get close to me again.

As we shared a cheesecake dessert covered in strawberries, I leaned across the table to kiss my date.

The dessert was delicious but not as good as her cannoli.

I smiled and thought to myself, "Yep, I'm spoiled already."

About the Author

Cheryl Powell, (writing under pen name Cheryl Denise Bannerman), is a multi-genre author of three successful works of fiction, a motivational speaker, and CEO. She resides in Orlando, Florida, where she runs a virtual Training and Development company, GC Learning Services LLC dba Learn2Engage, which she founded in 1996.

"My mother introduced me to books at an early age and encouraged me to not only read but also write. I remember having my first poem published in a collective book of poetry at the age of only 13. And when my mother wasn't working, I would read her my short stories, soaking in her edits and feedback like a sponge. Even at an early age, I was searching for perfection in my writings."

Through the trials and tribulations of her life, she has learned to heal through her writing. One of the few female authors to introduce topics of social concern within 'fictional' stories, her books draw from the most intimate life experiences and include characters who have been victims of child molestation and domestic violence, and who suffer from depression and various other addictions. For example, her second book, Words Never Spoken, which just won the 2018 Book Excellence Award, is a self-help, poetry, chapter-book about a woman who escaped an abusive relationship, and even includes self-reflection journal pages for readers to document their feelings and begin healing.

Her goal in life is to keep writing and continue helping victims of Domestic Abuse/Violence, Grief and ANON family groups, and Corporate Health and Wellness groups, to heal through words — encouraging them to 'write the pain' via journaling, and expressing themselves through short stories, songs, and poetry.

What Did You Think of A Bloody Stiletto, Cold Lasagna, and a Bestseller?

First of all, thank you for purchasing this book, *A Bloody Stiletto, Cold Lasagna, and a Bestseller*. I know you could have picked any number of books to read, but you picked this book, and for that, I am extremely grateful.

I hope that it added value and quality to your everyday life. If so, it would be awesome if you could share this book with your friends and family by posting to social media.

If you enjoyed this book and found some benefit in reading this, I would like to hear from you and hope that you could take some time to post a review on Amazon. Your feedback and support will help me to greatly improve my writing craft for future projects and make this book even better.

Visit the web site at www.bannermanbooks.com for contact information.

I want you, the reader, to know that your opinion is very important to me and hope that you will check out my other works of fiction:

Title	*Category/Genre*
Words Never Spoken	*Women's Inspirational/Poetry*
A Killer's Reflection	*Erotic Psychological Thriller/Serial Killer*
Black Child to Black Woman	*Women's Fiction/Urban Fiction/Family Saga*
Cats, Cannolis, and a Curious Kidnapping	*Book 1 of the Anna Romano Mystery Series*
Family Ties, Missing Organs, and Champagne	*Book 3 of a Cozy, Culinary Mystery Series*